THE LEGEND OF WHISKEY CITY

Book Three
in
The Whiskey City
Series

THE LEGEND OF WHISKEY CITY

Book Three
in
The Whiskey City
Series

•

ROBIN GIBSON

AVALON BOOKS
THOMAS BOUREGY AND COMPANY, INC.
401 LAFAYETTE STREET
NEW YORK, NEW YORK 10003

PRINTED IN THE UNITED STATES OF AMERICA
ON ACID-FREE PAPER
BY HADDON CRAFTSMEN, SCRANTON, PENNSYLVANIA

To my sister, Mona

Chapter One

Ready to drop from our saddles, we were beat as we rode up to Whiskey City. Even though not one light shone in the whole town, we could clearly see the place bathed in the moonlight. Not that there was much to see, just one lone street with buildings on either side. We called this home and weren't expecting any trouble. 'Course, knowing the folks of Whiskey City, we shoulda been ready for just about anything. As it was, the bullets that screamed at us took us totally by surprise.

There were eight of us in the party, returning from what had to be the worst cattle-buying trip in history. Somehow, we'd got tied up with a pack of ornery orphans and a band of vicious outlaws. A deadly combination, you'd have to admit. Why, we'd practically had to blast our way out of that country.

1

We'd been on the trail home for days now and were hot, tired, and sore. With the town in sight, we had let our guards down.

Well, when them bullets whipped past our heads, you can bet that we woke right up. We flopped out of our saddles like crickets off a hot skillet. Even the three women jumped down and hugged the dirt, covering their heads.

"Who goes there?" a shaky voice called from the livery stable. "Speak up, 'fore I blast somebody."

When he heard that voice, old man Wiesmulluer pushed himself to his feet. "Burdett, you crazy fool!" he roared with enough wind power to push a wagon uphill. "Put that gun down before you hurt someone."

"Karl, is that you?" Sam Burdett, our burly blacksmith, called, a hesitation in his voice. "How do I know it's really you?"

"What did he drink?" I heard Wiesmulluer grumble under his breath. Now old man Wiesmulluer had never been known for having patience. He'd built himself a nice ranch and he done it by bulling over or through anything in his way. Anything that got in his way or slowed him down infuriated the old coot. He was sure enough mad now. He kicked a rock and ground his fist into his palm. He was frothing at the mouth and ready to tear a chunk outta Burdett's backside.

With a heavy sigh I stepped in front of Wiesmulluer. "All right, I'm the sheriff, I'll handle this," I told him, trying to sound stern. I turned to Burdett. "Now, what's all this nonsense? How come you shot at us?"

"I didn't know it was you," Burdett declared.

"Who in Cooley's kingdom did you think it would be?" old man Wiesmulluer roared, the veins in his forehead about to bust open.

"Cimarron Bob," Burdett replied, dragging his rifle behind him as he shuffled out of the barn. "I've been standing guard every night for over a week, now. I swear, all this damp night air is playing hob with my gout. To say nothing of the sniffles I went and caught."

"Wait a minute," I said, cutting him off. Burdett always had something or other ailing him, and to tell the truth, I was tired of hearing about them. "You said Cimarron Bob. You mean the New Mexico badman?"

"You got porridge in your ears, boy?" Burdett bellered, and I could tell he was sore because I cut him off. "Of course, I said Cimarron Bob. I'm supposed to be watching for him right now."

"I think he's been burning locoweed in his forge again," Wiesmulluer grumbled as he helped his wife, Marie, to her feet. "What ever possessed you to stay out here all night watching for him?"

"'Cause he's a-comin' here!" Burdett sputtered, his eyes wide and wild. He wiped his mouth quickly on the back of his hand. "He's coming to kill Teddy!"

Now, I'd been helping my fiancée, Miss Edwinia Wiesmulluer, to her feet, but when I heard that Cimarron Bob was coming here after me, I dropped her hand and spun around to face Burdett. "What?" I screamed. "Who told you that?"

"The stage driver, Josh Reynolds. He heard it in the saloon over at Central City," Burdett replied.

"Oh well, now, that's reliable information," Marie Wiesmulluer scoffed as she dusted herself off. "Heaven knows, you can't believe everything you hear in a saloon."

That shut everybody up—except for Eddy. "Teddy!" she snapped, and that's when it finally dawned on me that I'd dropped her in the dirt. Fully expecting her to wallop me one, I hunched my shoulders and pasted a cheesy grin on my face as I turned to face her. She sat flat on her caboose in the dusty street. And believe me, the fire in her black eyes was enough to put gray hairs on your head.

"Sorry about that," I said, reaching down and hauling her to her feet. "It just startled me a little."

Eddy stepped up close to me, and for a second, I thought she was going to smile and forgive me. Instead, she made a face and stomped my toes. "Learn to watch what you are doing," she barked, her skirts snapping as she turned her back on me.

Mr. Claude helped his wife to her feet and managed to do it without dropping her. "I don't understand. Who is this Cimarron Bob?" he asked, his French accent having a hard time with the name.

"Well, I never met him, but I've heard tell of him for years," I said, my brow furrowing as I tried to recall what I'd heard about the man. "He's some kind of paid killer for the big cattle outfits, I think," I said, and glanced over at my partner, Bobby Stamper. In his wilder days, before he married Betsy Wiesmulluer,

Bobby had been a bank robber. I swear, that boy musta covered a lot of territory, 'cause he seemed to know everybody. Well, everybody with a shady past, anyway. "Did you ever come across him?" I asked.

Bobby smiled and shrugged. "I never bumped into the man face-to-face, but I sure heard a lot of stories. Way I heard it, he'd kill anybody or anything for a price."

"Teddy never done anything in his whole life," Betsy said, and I glared at her. Shoot, I'd done lots, I thought to myself. I was sheriff in these parts, and once I won a pie-eating contest. 'Course, being the biggest man in these parts helped with that. "Why would this man want to kill Teddy?" Betsy asked, looking from one face to another, but nobody had any bright ideas about that.

And before anyone could come up with a response, the banker, Mr. Andrews, rushed up toting a shotgun. "Did you get him? I heard shots," he bleated, waving the shotgun under our noses as he skidded to a stop. "Oh, it's only you," he grumbled, seeing us.

"Glad to see you too," I said, chuckling to myself as I gently pushed the shotgun barrel to where it pointed at the sky instead of my head. "Look, folks, we ain't gonna solve it tonight. Everybody go on to bed," I said, uncomfortable with all the attention.

"What about Cimarron Bob?" Burdett asked, fidgeting and worrying like a mother hen. "Somebody should stand guard and keep a lookout for him."

"I doubt if even the mighty Cimarron Bob could slip into my hotel room and shoot me in my sleep,"

I said. I shrugged off his concerns, but inside, I was touched. For years, I'd been helping Mr. Burdett in his livery and blacksmith shop, but I had no idea that he cared so much about me. A warm, rosy feeling spread through me as I looked at my circle of friends. Let Mister Cimarron Bob come. With these folks standing by my side, he wouldn't stand a chance.

"But what about the town?" Burdett wined, cutting through my thoughts. "Suppose he shows up and starts burning the town?" he squawked, throwing vinegar on my rosy feeling. Here I thought he was worried about me, but all he cared about was his little shop.

"Burdett's right," Andrews said, pushing up to me. "We have a lot invested in this town. We can't afford to have some wild-eyed badman burn it down around us."

"Wouldn't be no crying shame if he burned the whole blamed town. Most of it is falling down already," Wiesmulluer complained.

Well, he was sure enough right about that. The buildings in Whiskey City were in sad shape. 'Course, I reckon that's to be expected in a place where the folks don't know how to handle their blasting powder. The folks in this town had blown more holes in the buildings than ten Cimarron Bobs ever could. Still, they paid me to be sheriff, so I reckoned I had to do something.

I squeezed Burdett's shoulder and punched Andrews on the arm. "Don't you folks worry about a thing. If this feller Cimarron Bob shows up, I'll handle him. Your property is perfectly safe.''

Andrews rolled his eyes and walked away, cussing under his breath. From the way the others trotted off, I don't reckon they had all the confidence in the world in my ability to do the job. I guess the fact that I'd went broke trying to work the place my parents had left me when they passed on didn't give them a lot of confidence in my ability. Well, I'd danged sure show them.

Burdett scowled, shoving his hands down in his pockets as he kicked the ground. ''Aw, all right,'' he finally muttered. He bent down to snag his rifle out of the dust. ''But I'm warning you. You let my place get burned down and I'm gonna flog you like a stray pup!'' he blustered, waving that rifle under my nose.

''You can't talk to Teddy like that!'' Eddy shouted, fire snapping in her black eyes. She doubled up her fists and got right up in Burdett's face.

I grabbed her by the arms and pulled her back before she could haul back and clock the blacksmith, which she was liable to do. ''It's OK, Eddy; I can handle this,'' I assured her. ''Why don't you go get some sleep. We'll talk about it in the morning.''

''Oh, all right,'' she said, jerking away from me and shaking her fist at Burdett. ''I'm going to the hotel, but you best watch what you say, buster,'' she told Burdett. She gave me a peck on the cheek and said sweetly, ''Good night, Teddy.'' Turning around, she branded Burdett with a seething glance, then marched

toward the hotel. She stomped right past Burdett, forc-
ing the burly blacksmith to jump back out of her way.

Burdett started to mumble something under his
breath, but I laid my big paw on his shoulder, cutting
his mumblings off at the pass. He smiled weakly up
at me. "She shore takes after her paw," he muttered,
and I had to agree with that. Dragging the butt of his
rifle in the dirt, he shuffled off in the direction of his
house. He didn't go four paces before he stopped and
looked back. "By the way, I could use a hand. With
all this night duty, I've shore got behind in my work.
I was wondering . . . well, if you don't have anything
better to do."

"I'll come by tomorrow and lend a hand," I promised tiredly. I was plumb frazzled from the long ride
and all the scrambling about tonight and didn't really
feel up to helping him, but I wanted the money. I was
just starting to realize how much stuff me and Eddy
had to buy before we got married. I mean, I could get
by on about anything, but Eddy wanted stuff like a
new stove and dishes. In fact, she wanted more dishes
than a body could use in a week. Now, I never saw
the need for half the stuff she thought we had to have,
but if she wanted it, I wanted her to have it. Shaking
my head and feeling old and tired, I ambled over to
the hotel where I found Bobby sitting on the bench
outside waiting on me.

Bobby stood up as I approached, and for one of the
few times in his life he wore a serious expression. "I
didn't want to say anything in front of the ladies, but
if Cimarron Bob is after you, you got big problems.

So far he's nailed every man he ever went after. It's a matter of pride with him now. If I were you, I'd stay in town, and if you have to leave town, don't go alone.''

''Aw, we don't even know if he's coming. Likely all of this is just a bunch of loose-mouthed talk,'' I scoffed.

''Sure, but if it ain't?'' Bobby asked quietly, and I didn't have an answer. ''Look, Teddy, most of the fellers Cimarron Bob killed never even knew he was in the country. All I'm saying is just be careful. I'm going to write a few letters and see if Bob's really coming and maybe who hired him.''

''You know who to write?'' I asked doubtfully. Now, it wasn't so much that I doubted whether Bobby knew who to write, but that he actually knew somebody that could read.

Bobby had no such doubts. He smiled broadly, clapping me on the back as we walked inside the hotel. ''When you are on the dodge like I was, you meet a lot of interesting folks,'' he admitted, a sly, smirking sound in his voice. ''Me and Betsy are going out to the ranch to work on our house tomorrow,'' he said, turning serious again. He placed both hands on my shoulders and looked me square in the eyes. ''You just watch your back and be careful. If you have to leave town send for me, or get Turley to go with you.''

''Turley!'' I howled, rolling my eyes. ''Come on, Bobby, that old goat drives me crazy. I'd just about soon get shot,'' I declared. And believe me, I wasn't stretching the truth much. Turley Simmons was a bigger pain in the backside than a handful of sandburs in your drawers.

Bobby laughed, shaking his head. "He's a handful, all right, but he's trapped up and down this country and got along in wild country for a long time. With him along, nobody's going to get a good shot at you."

"Oh yeah? Well, I was raised in wild country myself," I allowed. "I reckon I can take care of myself."

"Sure you can, but two sets of eyes are better than one," Bobby replied. He squeezed my shoulder and shifted his feet. "I never had a partner that I liked and trusted before. I don't want you to get yourself killed before we get this ranch going."

Having spoke his piece, Bobby hurried upstairs. I watched him step into his room, then plopped down on the stairs. I didn't really think Cimarron Bob was coming after me and couldn't think of any reason why someone would want me dead. Still, what Bobby said made sense. It would be best to go easy until he checked things out. Rubbing the back of my neck, I stared at the warped stairs. When was life going to get simple? It never would, I supposed as I hauled myself to my feet and tromped upstairs.

The next morning, I had breakfast with Eddy. We talked about where we would build our new house and what we would need to furnish it. After we ate, I walked her out to her parents' wagon. I watched until the wagon was out of sight, then trudged down to Burdett's shop.

Turley Simmons sat on a stump, chewing on a piece of straw. "What are you doing here?" I asked gruffly.

Turley's face split into a toothy grin. "Just came down here to keep you company," he replied cheerfully.

"I'm going to be working," I informed him stiffly. "I don't need no company."

"Well, I'll just watch you work," Turley announced. "I always liked watching somebody work. Never took to the stuff myself, but I sure admire watching."

"That's for sure," I grumbled. "I know Bobby Stamper sent you here to watch over me, but I don't need a nurse."

"Maybe, but I'll stick around and make sure the bogeyman don't get you." Turley slapped his thigh and broke into a cackling laugh. "Be a downright shame to lose a fine, upstanding man like you."

For a week, I worked from sunup to sundown. I made horseshoes, put some iron rims on Andrews's buggy wheels, and made a plow for Mr. Claude. By the end of the week, my nerves were frazzled. Between Turley's stories and Mr. Burdett's complaining, I'd took just about all the company I could stand. By then, I'd done decided to take a couple of days and do some prospecting. There had been gold found in these parts from time to time. As a matter of fact, Turley found himself a pile of it. I figured if other folks found gold, maybe I could sniff out a little my ownself.

I gathered my tools early Saturday morning, then stopped down at the store to lay in some groceries. Gid Stevens, who owned the place, stood behind the counter, and I had to stop and knuckle my eyes a couple of times to make sure I saw him. I just couldn't get used to seeing him here. Before he started hanging around old widder Winkler, Gid never stayed in the store. Folks just came in and helped themselves and wrote what they took on their bill. 'Course, since Gid teamed up with Iris Winkler things had sure changed. That woman was frugal as a cur dog, and just about as friendly. If ol' Gid wasn't careful, she'd have him down here day and night. And she'd expect him to work while he was here; Iris didn't stand for any loafing around.

I reckon the same notion had occurred to Gid because he looked sour as cactus berries. He hardly even looked up as I came into the store. He just slurped his coffee, ignoring me.

I roamed the store, picking up some beans, coffee, and a slab of bacon. "You going on a trip, Teddy?" Gid asked as I plopped my goods on the counter.

"Yeah, I'm going to do a little prospecting," I replied as Gid struggled to tally up my bill.

Gid's hand jerked so hard that he snapped the lead in his pencil. "Do you think that is wise?" he asked quickly. "Suppose Cimarron Bob shows up while you're gone? A man like that, there's no telling what he might do if he found the sheriff was out of town."

"He ain't coming," I said assuringly, waving off his concerns. "It's been over a week. If he was coming, he'd already be here."

With Gid still blabbering and worrying, I gathered my provisions and walked out of the store. As I packed my gear on my horse, I took notice of the day: bright, sunny, and peaceful. Despite the beauty, I felt a twinge of sadness. Summer was almost over, and winter was on the way. Even now, the mornings were cool and I had to slip on my jacket.

I rode out of town with big ambitions and high hopes, but by the time I pitched camp, those were long gone. I'd panned, dug, and hunted up and down the country, but I hadn't found enough gold to buy a piece of used chewing tobacco.

As I pitched my camp and fixed supper, I realized how much I had missed Eddy this week. Just closing my eyes, I could picture her black hair and her flashing smile. In my mind, I could hear her bubbling laugh.

Puttering around my camp, it came to me that tomorrow was Sunday. If I recalled right, Eddy's mom always laid out a healthy spread for Sunday dinner. Now, I could do some more prospecting in the morning, working my way over toward the Wiesmulluer ranch. If I worked things right, I could mosey in there just in time to help them polish off that Sunday dinner, then spend the rest of the day with Eddy.

I looked down at the mush of beans and bacon I fixed for myself and decided that notion was a right good one. I'm a good-sized man and it takes a lot of chow to keep me going, more than I could cook for myself. Besides, the Wiesmulluers were going to be my in-laws. I should get to know them better. My mind jumping back and forth between visions of Eddy and Marie Wiesmulluer's peach cobbler, I spread out my blankets.

I took off my gunbelt, boots, and hat and dropped them into a pile. Fighting a yawn, I slipped into bed, rolling the blankets tight around me, fighting the cool night air. I was just about to drift off to sleep when I heard it.

For a second I lay there, my mind drowsily trying to identify the sound. Then I heard it again—the rustle of bushes and the sound of something rubbing against rough tree bark. Somebody was cat-footing it up to my camp!

I shot a glance at my horse, who stood rigid as a stone statue, his ears pricked at attention. My eyes moved in a slow arch in front of me as I carefully tried to untangle myself from my blankets. A shadow moved in front of me. For a fleeting second, the shadow was framed in the moonlight and I saw it clear—a man, a hulk of a man, carrying a rifle. Cimarron Bob! He'd found me!

Never taking my eyes from the shadow, I eased one hand from the blanket, reaching for my shooter. I couldn't reach it! As I slapped around desperately for my pistol, the shadow raised his rifle, taking dead aim.

Chapter Two

The man in the shadows aimed the rifle straight at me calling out in the dark. "Teddy Cooper? Is that you?"

I thought I recognized that grating voice, but I still didn't trust him, nor the rifle he carried. "Yeah, it's me," I called softly, my fingers still exploring the ground in search of my pistol. Finally my fingers found the leather of the gunbelt and drug it to me. "Whadda you want?" I called out, easing the weapon out of the holster.

"Teddy, it's me, Luther," the shadow hissed. "You know, Bobby's friend."

I groaned. I shoulda known. One of Bobby's old outlaw buddies. We'd met Luther on our cattle-buying trip, and while I liked the big outlaw, I didn't care for him waking me up. Not to mention scaring the bejeebers outta me. ''Come on up to the fire,'' I said sourly and poked my pistol down in my jeans. I stirred up the fire and slid the coffeepot onto the coals. ''What's on your mind?'' I asked as the big outlaw eased quietly up to the fire.

''I heard something you ought to know about,'' Luther said, holding the rifle in the crook of his arm. ''I heard somebody went and hired Cimarron Bob. I reckon he's on his way here to kill you.''

''We heard the rumors,'' I said in acknowledgment, squatting by the fire and extending my hands to the flames.

Luther chuckled a rich, deep laugh. ''I thought you might have. That's why I came up to your camp careful like. Would be a shame to get myself shot, now that I've decided to go straight,'' Luther said, moving gracefully as he squatted beside me. ''You might want to be more careful your ownself. If I'd been Cimarron Bob, you'd be dead now.''

I felt a nerve jump in my face. He was right about that. ''I never really believed he was coming,'' I said lamely. ''How sure are you of what you heard?''

''There ain't no secrets where I been,'' Luther said with a shrug. ''I was afraid he'd beat me here.'' Luther stirred the fire with a stick. ''Cimarron Bob don't come cheap. Somebody wants you dead awful bad. You musta stepped on some big toes. Any idea whose?''

''Bobby asked me the same question, and I've been thinking about it the last few days. I can't think of anyone who might have a grudge agin me, much less anybody that would go to the bother of hiring a man like Cimarron Bob.''

''That ain't all,'' Luther said quietly. He took the pot off the fire and poured himself a cup of coffee. ''They hired another man. You ever hear of a jasper named Nick Oakley?''

I scoured my brain, but I couldn't dab a loop on the memory of an Oakley. ''Never heard of him,'' I decided.

''He's in the same line of work as Cimarron Bob. Oakley's not as slick as Bob, but he sure enjoys the work. I'd say he enjoys it a lot.''

I looked down into my cup, my spirits black as the coffee. ''Well, I don't know what I can do except handle the trouble when it comes.''

Luther started to take a drink, pausing to give me a long look over the rim of his coffee cup. ''You could try and find out who's behind all of this,'' he suggested.

''I don't know,'' I said hesitantly. ''Shoot, I wouldn't even know how to go about it.''

''I could do it,'' Luther said, then explained quickly. ''Look, Teddy, I know you're a right handy young feller and one ring-tailed fighter, but you can't win at this the way you're going at it. Even if you do beat Bob and Oakley, there will be more. You want to kill a man every week?''

''No, but what can I do?''

''I can find out who's hiring these men. Don't think for a second that if you handle Oakley and Cimarron

Bob that will be the end of it. Believe me, there will be more.''

I stood up, pacing behind the fire. I reckon Luther was right, but I wondered why he would be so anxious to help me. ''Why would you go to all this fuss for me? I hardly know you.''

''I like you. Ain't that enough?'' Luther smiled, his big square teeth flashing. I frowned, not buying one bit of it. I could smell manure when it was handed to me. ''All right, all right,'' Luther said with a small laugh. ''I need a favor from you. I figure if I find out who is sending these men to kill you, then you would owe me a favor.''

''What kind of a favor?'' I asked warily.

Luther's smile deepened and he took another swig of his coffee. ''I'll tell you about that when the time is ripe. In the meantime, you just be sure and keep yourself alive. You ain't no good to me dead. Hang around Bobby. He's slicker than a greased otter. I swear, that boy must have eyes in the back of his head not to have got himself caught after some of the stunts he pulled,'' Luther said, chuckling as he tossed the rest of his coffee on the ground.

''This favor you want from me, is it going to get me in trouble?'' I asked as the big outlaw rose and crossed to his horse.

Luther stopped, grinning back at me. ''You're already in trouble, Teddy,'' he said, his booming laugh echoing back at me. I could still hear his laugh as he mounted and rode away. ''Tell Bobby, I ain't forgot about the money he owes me.''

After Luther left, I sat by the fire, drinking coffee. I kept going over everything I'd done in the past few years. For the life of me, I couldn't think of anyone who might want me dead. Groaning, I rubbed my temples. All this thinking was giving me a headache, so I gave it up.

I kicked dirt over my fire and crawled back into my blankets. I tried to go to sleep but couldn't, which was strange for me. I'm a man that enjoys his sleep, but tonight I heard a threat in each little sound. Every time I closed my eyes, I saw a faceless assassin drawing a bead on me.

I don't know when I finally fell asleep, but I didn't wake up until way past daybreak. Still groggy from sleeping late, I yawned constantly as I gathered my stuff and broke camp. In the bright light of day, what me and Luther talked about didn't stack up to much. With the darkness pressing in on you and the wind moaning through the trees, a body's imagination gets to running hog-wild. But with the birds singing and the sun shining this morning, the threat of some faceless gunman didn't seem so real.

Still, I was careful as I pointed my horse toward the Wiesmulluer ranch. Since I'd slept so late, I didn't stop for any prospecting. Even so, I barely made it by noon.

As I rode up to the house, I saw old man Wiesmulluer, Bobby Stamper, and Turley Simmons sitting on the porch. When I saw Turley, I almost swung my horse around and bolted out of there. Now, it wasn't that I didn't like Turley, I just didn't like the fact that he was always teasing me.

I might have turned and run, but they had already seen me. The whole bunch flocked off the porch like a flock of chickens going after a feed bucket.

Eddy rushed out of the kitchen, nearly bowling me over with a big hug. "Oh, Teddy. Where in creation have you been? We've all been terribly worried," she whispered in my ear.

"I was out doing a little prospecting."

Eddy stepped back, her hands on her hips. "Theodore Cooper! Have you lost your mind? There's a hired killer out there looking for you!"

"Aw, I was being extra careful," I replied, trying to shrug away her fears, but I could see it wasn't going to work. "I figured to make some extra money, so we can buy the things we need after we are married."

Eddy clucked her tongue and rolled her eyes. She started to speak, then pushed my horse away as he tried to nuzzle her. "Well, that's real smart," she finally said tightly. "I'm sure we will have a nice wedding if you're dead."

Marie Wiesmulluer stepped to the screen door. "Eddy, leave the poor man alone and come help me set the table for dinner. You men go get washed up. It's almost ready." As everyone jumped to do as she asked, Marie stepped outside, cutting me out of the bunch. "It's so nice of you to join us, Teddy," she said sweetly; then a stern expression crossed her face. "But Eddy is right, you should be more careful, at least until this horrible man Cimarron Bob is captured.''

''Yes, ma'am,'' I replied, hanging my head.

Marie laughed and shoved me in the direction of the pump. ''Now, go get washed up and come in for dinner.''

Well, that sounded like a first-rate idea to me, but I didn't get much of a chance to enjoy the dinner. Not with everybody harping on me. Even Bobby took to lecturing me like a schoolmarm. Yeah, and after all the danged fool stunts he's pulled. I was sorely disappointed. I didn't even get a chance to speak with Eddy alone.

She rode back to town with me, but even then we didn't get much of a chance to talk. Turley rode with us, and with Turley around nobody ever gets more than a word or two in edgeways. 'Course, talking wasn't exactly all I had in mind. But it just wasn't meant to be. We said our good-nights and went to bed.

The next morning I was up and around early, but I wasn't in a good mood, that was for sure. I marched straight down to the blacksmith shop, feeling the need to bang on something this morning. Even so, Turley beat me to the shop. He sat in the dirt, calmly chewing on a piece of jerky as he rested his back against a wagon wheel. ''What are you doing here?'' I growled, eyeing him warily.

''Keeping an eye on you,'' Turley replied cheerfully.

I shot a surly scowl at him. ''Well, you can just

forget about that. I can take care of myself!'' I allowed.

''Don't doubt it for a minute,'' Turley agreed, but his mocking grin said something different. ''But Eddy done paid me a dollar to keep you out of trouble. Now, I reckon that job is worth more than a dollar, but I like Eddy so I gave her a bargin. Besides, if Cimarron Bob shows up, I wouldn't want to miss all the fun.''

''There ain't gonna be no fun here. If you don't have business, you can just move along. I got work to do, and I don't need you hanging around playing wet nurse.''

Turley never even turned a hair, he just popped the last piece of jerky in his mouth and climbed to his feet. ''I guess I best take a little ride and see what's lurking in the shadows.'' He grinned at me, pointing to a small rise just outside of town. ''You ever stop to think what a good man with a rifle could do from there? No? I didn't reckon you did. Just think about it; you could be hammering away when, wham!'' he shouted and slapped my chest. ''You're dead, Teddy.''

For a second, my breath caught in my throat and a slimy feeling crawled up my legs. I stared at the spot, my throat dry all of a sudden. Turley laughed, whacking me on the back. ''Aw, cheer up. He might miss.'' Turley walked away, mumbling to himself. '' 'Course, nobody ever heard of Cimarron Bob missing, but then I don't reckon it's impossible. Sure, everybody misses from time to time. 'Course, you make a mighty big target.'' Turley climbed up on his horse and looked back at me, his eyes shining with mirth. "Yeah, I reckon he might miss."

Now, let me tell you, that was a real comfort to me. "Get out of here. I don't want to hear your opinions," I said, growling, but I couldn't keep my mind from what Turley said.

I started to work, but my eyes kept straying to the knoll Turley had pointed out. I managed to mash my thumb a couple of times by not paying attention.

I was sucking my thumb, trying to ease the pain of my last mishap, when the shadow of a horse and rider fell across my workbench. That danged Turley! How was I supposed to get any work done with him flocking around like a buzzard over a downed steer? Why I had a notion to . . .

That notion wilted and died as I raised my eyes. My throbbing thumb slid from my mouth as my jaw sagged open. I couldn't see much of the rider's face; his hat was pulled low and the sun was directly behind him, glaring in my eyes. No, sir, I couldn't see much of his face, but I knew it wasn't Turley. In a flash, I knew who it was—Cimarron Bob!

"You Teddy Cooper?" the rider asked in a dry, rasping voice that reminded me of the buzz of a rattler. Unable to speak, I nodded my head slowly, my eyes widening as his hand fell to his gun. "I came here to kill you."

Chapter Three

"My name is Cimarron Bob Williams, and I came here to kill you," he repeated, his fingers tickling the polished butt of his pistol.

"Why?" I croaked around the lump in my throat. I spread my arms, trying to look harmless as possible, while my eyes whipped from side to side, scanning the street for Turley. Where in the world was that old bag of bones, anyway? Some protector he turned out to be. "Why would you want to kill me?"

"That there ain't none of your business," Bob said quietly.

"None of my business!" I howled without thinking. "Why, you danged old skinflint, I oughta yank you off that horse and flog you raw!"

"Anytime you're ready, boy," Bob replied evenly.

All of a sudden, my rage plumb melted. "Ah, look,

24

Mr. Bob, y-you don't want to d-do this,'' I said with a stutter, trying to keep the shake out of my voice. ''You don't have any r-reason for w-wanting to kill me.''

Cimarron Bob chuckled, a dry sound that made the hair on the back of my neck stand up. ''You're wrong about that, lawman. I've got ten thousand reasons.'' Bob smiled down at me. ''Now, I reckon if you want to, you can go for your gun. Not that it'll do you any good, but you can try.''

Moving slowly, I stepped away from the work-bench. With the sun no longer directly behind him, I saw his face. My eyes snapped wide open as I stared up at him in shock. Cimarron Bob was an old man!

''What are you gaggling at, you overgrown saddle sore?'' Bob snarled. ''Why, I got a notion to whip you before I kill you!''

I laughed. I didn't want to laugh at the old man. I just couldn't help it. The snicker just kinda snuck out of my mouth. Cimarron Bob's wrinkled face turned red, and he went for his gun. I didn't even draw my own pistol, I was so shocked by his speed. Now, it wasn't that he was so blindingly fast, just the opposite, pitifully slow. Why, I've seen corpses move quicker. He clawed at his gun, finally dragging the thing out of the holster. Then his whole arm spasmed, and he dropped that Colt into the dust.

His hand bent and twisted into the shape of a claw, Cimarron Bob stared at that hogleg. Holding his hand to his chest, he met my gaze, a look of defiance in his watery blue eyes. "Well, what are you waiting for, an invitation? Shoot, you filthy dog!" he raged.

His words snapped me out of the stupor I'd been in. I started to draw my weapon, then stopped, unsure what to do. "Shoot!" Bob roared, spitting and sputtering. When I only stared up at him, he tried to kick me, but only succeeded in losing his balance and toppling off his horse. I rushed over to help him, but he rolled over, using the stirrup to pull himself to his feet. He picked up his pistol with both hands and pointed it at me, but the gun wasn't cocked. Cursing again, he had to put the gun between his legs to cock it. While he struggled to pull the hammer back, Eddy charged him from behind. She must have come from the kitchen in the hotel, 'cause she carried a big ol' iron skillet. And believe me, she had it pulled back behind her head, ready to smack something.

"Eddy, no!" I shouted, but I was too late. Cimarron Bob tried to turn, but he was too slow as well. He did manage to duck enough so the frying pan didn't clobber him over the head, but it did wallop him square in the back. With a bleat of pain, he tumbled awkwardly to the ground.

Her face flushing and her black eyes snapping fire, Eddy rared back with the skillet, ready to whack him another time. "Eddy, don't!" I shouted and grabbed her around the waist. I lifted her clean off the ground; then, spinning around, I pulled her across the fallen Bob and plopped her down on the ground. Keeping an eye on her, I stooped down and snatched Cimarron

Bob's gun, then helped the old-timer to his feet. "Are you all right, sir?"

Bob twisted out of my grasp, slapping my hands frantically. "Get your hands off of me, you sorry son of a pup!"

Feeling a rush of anger, I placed my hands on my hips, glaring at the old man. "I was just trying to help," I said tersely.

"Yeah? Well, I don't need any help from a stack of meadow muffins like you," he said with a growl and kicked my shin. "Now give me my gun back," he barked, his whole body creaking like a cemetery gate as he grabbed at the pistol.

I jerked the gun back out of his reach, holding the hogleg over my head as I looked at him through slitted eyes. "Are you going to try and shoot me again?"

Bob cussed a blue streak, kicking the ground in disgust. "You darn betcha, I am! And this time I'll get the job done!" he thundered.

Her hands crossed over her chest, Eddy got nose-to-nose with the old man. "Why do you want to kill Teddy?"

"Who rattled your cage, sister?" Bob growled, and I had to drag Eddy back before she beat him up. "If you want to say something, tell tree trunk there to give me my gun back."

"I don't think I can do that," I said, fighting to hold Eddy back.

"Think?" Bob hooted. "Between the two of you, you couldn't think your way out of an outhouse. Now give me my shooter back."

I shook my head, and for an instant I thought he would start a row over the deal, but finally he growled, spun around, and walked toward his horse.

"Where do you think you are going?" I called, but Cimarron Bob ignored me, muttering under his breath as he kept going to his horse. "Hey, you! Come back here!" I yelled.

"Aw, blow it out your snoot!" Bob shot back, his back snapping and popping like the Fourth of July as he bent down to pick up his reins.

"I want to ask you a few questions," I said stubbornly. "Now, you can answer them here and now, or after you spend a couple of days in jail."

"You can't throw me in jail. I ain't done nothing wrong."

"You tried to kill the sheriff. We sorta frown on that in these parts," I informed him.

Cimarron Bob snorted, waving his hand back at me. He poked his foot in the stirrup and started to mount, but about halfway his whole body seemed to just lock up. He hung that way for an instant, then he toppled stiffly to the ground. He lit on the ground as stiff as an ironing board.

We rushed over to the old man as he struggled to regain his feet. "Are you all right?" I asked, helping him sit up.

"I could use a drink," he mumbled.

"Sure," I mumbled while Eddy brushed the dirt from his back. I took the tin cup that hung from the pump and filled it with water. "Here you go," I said, hurrying the cup back over to him.

His veined hand trembled slightly as he took the cup from my fingers. He took a swig, then spit water everywhere. "That's water!" he cried hoarsely.

"You said you wanted a drink," I accused.

"Why you smart-mouthed pup, giving a man water when he was expecting something else is enough to kill him," Cimarron Bob sputtered.

"I take it that you wanted something with a little kick to it?" Eddy said, a twinkle in her eye.

Bob shot her a hard look. "Well, shoot, yes." He cut his eyes to the sky and sighed heavily. "Between the two of them, they don't have the brain of a sparrow."

"You're awful sassy for a man in your position," I said, grumbling. "You're lucky I don't haul you into jail. I almost wish now I would have shot you!"

"Teddy!" Eddy exclaimed. "What a thing to say!"

Old Cimarron Bob hacked and spat on the ground. "I wish you woulda had the guts to shoot. That's what I came here for."

"What?" I screeched, not understanding him.

"Do them floppy things you call ears hanging off the side of your head work, boy?" Cimarron Bob growled. "I said I came here so you could kill me!"

"Why do you want Teddy to kill you?" Eddy asked, sitting down beside the old man and rubbing his shoulders gently.

For a second, Cimarron Bob's face softened and a look of sadness snuck into his eyes. "Dang, woman, I'm eighty-three years old," he said bitterly. "If you ask me, that's long enough for anyone to live."

"But why did you pick me?" I asked, scratching my head.

"You got a price on your head. I figured that in case I got lucky, I needed to collect some money to eat on. Besides, I heard about you. You polished off Dutch Adkins and his boys. I heard you collared up Riley Hunt. I figured you could do the job, and I didn't want to get killed by some snot-nosed punk." He grumbled and rolled his eyes. "You sure were a big disappointment. You couldn't kill a bug with a stick. I guess I'll have to find somebody else."

Eddy glanced up at me, the look in her eyes telling me that she expected me to do something for the old skinflint. I sighed, knowing I'd break down and do it too. "That don't hardly sound reasonable to me. I reckon you should be thankful for every day you get," I told him.

Cimarron Bob laughed sarcastically, the laugh trailing off into a cough. "Grow up, boy," he said hacking. "I can't move, my bones ache. . . . Now, smarty-pants, tell me, what do I have to be thankful for?"

"Well, you're not a sheriff. Believe me, you can be thankful of that," I said, trying to lighten the old man up, but I was only half-joking. 'Course, Cimarron Bob didn't see any humor in it. He didn't even bother to respond. "Who put the bounty on my head?" I asked.

A ghost of a smile flitted across Cimarron Bob's weathered lips. "I can't tell you that. It wouldn't be ethical."

"Ethical!" I screamed, smacking my fist into my

palm. "What in the world do you know about ethics? You're a hired killer, for Pete's sake."

Eddy shot me a fiery glance and whacked my shoulder. "Theodore Cooper! You should be ashamed of yourself. You know better than to talk to your elders that way."

I bit my lip and grumbled under my breath. I mean, never mind that she clobbered him with a cast-iron skillet. "I'm sorry, Mr. Bob," I mumbled grudgingly.

"That's better," Eddy said tightly, then went to work on Cimarron Bob. "We also heard that a man named Nick Oakley was coming after Teddy. What do you know about that?" she demanded.

Cimarron Bob shrugged his sagging shoulders. "I don't know anything about that," he admitted, his head still hanging between his knees. All of a sudden, his head snapped up, them washed-out blue eyes blazing. I took a step back, seeing from the look on his face why Cimarron Bob had been feared for years. "So, they didn't think I was up to the job!" And let me tell you, for a man that claimed he couldn't move, Cimarron Bob sure shot to his feet. He wobbled for a second on creaking knees, his face blazing with rage. Without so much as a word, he snatched up his reins and stalked away.

"Hey, Mr. Bob!" I shouted, taking a step after him. "I'm not through with you yet."

Eddy tugged at my sleeve. "Oh, Teddy, let him go," she pleaded.

"He should go to jail!" I wiped my mouth and

ground my heel into the dust, staring after the old man. "He tried to kill me!"

Eddy laughed brightly and slapped my sleeve. "Don't be silly. That sweet old gentleman couldn't hurt a fly."

"Oh, yeah? What about all the men he's supposed to have killed over the years," I countered hotly.

Eddy laughed again, taking my arm and banging her head softly against my shoulder. "Pooh, you know how stories get started, and stretched way beyond the truth. Maybe Cimarron Bob has had some difficulties over the years, but then, who hasn't? I think he is just a lonely old man looking for some friendship."

I wasn't at all sure I believed all of that, but I shrugged off my doubts. I mean, the day I couldn't handle a rickety old coot like Cimarron Bob was the day they ought to plant me six feet under. Little did I know, that very thing was a distinct possibility.

Eddy and I strolled arm in arm down the street. My eyes kept straying over to Cimarron Bob as the old man limped painfully into the saloon. I didn't like having him running around loose. I mean, his body might be shot, but I don't reckon there was anything wrong with his mind. If he wanted to raise Cain, I figured he'd find a way to do it.

Eddy musta known what I was thinking, 'cause she laughed and pulled me toward the hotel. "Why don't you take me to dinner and forget about him?" she asked.

"I don't like him. What's more, I don't trust him neither," I grumbled, but I let her drag me up the street toward the café. At the door, I balked, glaring fiercely back at the saloon. "Why, I got a good notion to go back and toss him in the clink."

We sat down at a table and ordered our lunch. Mrs. Fowler, who ran the hotel, brought our grub. 'Course, I didn't get to eat any of it. No, sir, not one bite.

I was just fixin' to take my first bite when old man Wiesmulluer busted into the room, snorting and pawing like a bull in the ring. He skidded to a stop just inside the door, breathing fire and looking for somebody to charge. Well, I musta been wearing a red cape or something, 'cause no sooner did his eyes settle on me than he went off. "Teddy! I want a word with you," he thundered, his boots thudding loudly as he rushed over to us.

"Sit down. We were just getting ready to eat," I offered, eyeing him warily.

"I ain't got time and neither do you," Wiesmulluer roared, jerking me to my feet. "Somebody done stole a bunch of my cattle!"

Wiesmulluer rushed me out of the place so fast, I never even got a chance to say good-bye to Eddy, much less grab a bite or two from my meal. The way Wiesmulluer was ranting and raving, I clean forgot about Cimarron Bob and Nick Oakley.

Just shy of sundown, we reached the spot where his cattle had disappeared. As far as such things go, I reckon it was a right nice spot, a bowl-like depression dotted with trees and a waterhole in the center. We stopped our horses at the rim of the bowl, and I stepped down, handing my reins to the old man. "You stay here while I take a look," I told him.

Wiesmulluer cussed under his breath and looked up at the sky, but he stayed on his horse while I criss-crossed the area. I could see where about twenty head had been rounded up and held in the bowl. I found the outlaws' camp and could see where they had thrown the cattle and changed the brands.

"You figure it out?" Wiesmulluer asked, the sudden sound of his voice beside me making me jump out of my skin.

"They went off to the south," I said tersely. I was mad at him for sneaking up on me and mad at me for letting it happen.

"You figure that out all by yourself?" Wiesmulluer sneered. "Shoot! Any fool can see that."

Together, Wiesmulluer and I set out on the trail. The tracks were easy to follow, as the rustlers were moving fast, making no attempt to hide their tracks. As the sun slid behind the edge of the mountains, I wanted to stop, but Wiesmulluer would have none of that. He insisted that we push on. "That trail is as plain as a skirt on a sow and there will be a full moon tonight. We shouldn't have any trouble," he reasoned.

I done some muttering under my breath and pounded my fist into my thigh. I was tired and hungry enough to eat a mulehide. Wiesmulluer didn't pay any mind to my protest, so I followed him. Even though everything he had said was true, we still had a time sticking to the trail. Then we up and lost it.

We were riding through some trees, where the

moonlight didn't filter in, when we lost the tracks. As Wiesmulluer griped and grumbled, we got off our horses, looking for the trail on our hands and knees.

"Maybe we should camp here for the night," I suggested, and when the old man didn't blow his top, I pressed my argument. "We came a far piece tonight. I reckon we gained on them some. Come morning, we should be able to find the trail plumb easy."

Now, we may have been standing in the shadows, but I could still see the anger flash in his weather-beaten face. "Nothing doing," he said flatly. "We'll make some torches."

He struck a match, holding it high as he looked on the ground for some wood to use as torches. For a second, he was peacefully framed in the flickering yellow light. Then the crash of a rifle split the night air. I saw his jacket jump as the bullet thumped him hard in the chest. With a wheezing sigh, Wiesmulluer melted to the ground, the match burning out in his unfeeling fingers.

Chapter Four

As Karl fell to the ground, I drew my weapon and flopped down beside him. I gripped my pistol, staring into the darkness, trying to see where the shot came from. In the vague light, all I could see were gray lumps and hazy shapes.

Out of the corner of my eye, I could see Wiesmulluer's crumpled body. I couldn't tell if he was dead or alive, and I couldn't afford to move and find out. In this light, as long as I stayed still, I was invisible, just one shadow among hundreds of others, but if I moved, I would stand out like a dancing girl at a bachelor picnic.

I couldn't see my attackers, and they couldn't see me. It was a standoff; the first to move would be the first to die.

"Lester, Lester. I got him!" a shaky voice called

out excitedly from the dark. My eyes followed the sound of his voice, but couldn't spot the man.

"Shut up, Elmo," another voice hissed urgently. As the sound of his voice died away, an eerie silence descended on us, broken only by the low moan of the wind. The silence grated on my nerves and evidently it did the same to Lester. "You got the big one? You got that sheriff feller?"

Irritation sounded in Elmo's voice as he answered, "Sure I got him. You heard me say so, didn't you?"

While they jawed back and forth, I took a chance and moved. If I could get around behind them, I'd be in the driver's seat. I didn't really want to shoot them, but after what they did to Wiesmulluer, I wasn't going to rassle with my scruples if one of them wandered across my sights.

I moved with care, shifting my body slowly, inch by inch. I was just about to think I might get away with it when Lester let out a curse and snapped off a shot. The bullet smacked into the ground right in front of me. Startled, I let out a yelp, then froze in my tracks.

"I nailed him!" Lester screamed excitedly. "I nailed the old geezer!"

From the flash of his rifle, I had Lester's position pinpointed. I could even make out the fuzzy outline of his body. It was a long shot for a pistol, but I reckoned if I had to, I could get him. The only problem was, once I nixed Lester, the shots would give my position away and Elmo would turn me into a bean sieve real quick.

"Are you sure you got him?" Elmo called out, doubt sounding in his voice. "I don't see him."

"He tried to move and I plugged him," Lester maintained firmly. "I reckon he was trying to slip around behind us."

"Why, that sorry polecat!" Elmo howled. "Imagine that, trying to sneak up behind and ambush us. That ain't hardly neighborly."

I gritted my teeth and fought the temptation to bang my head against the ground. These two dimwits had set an ambush and we'd walked right into it. I wanted to jump up and rush them, but I didn't. I mean, these two might not be the sharpest jaspers to ever amble by, but having their heads packed full of sawdust instead of brains didn't affect their shooting eyes any. They'd fired two shots in poor light and hit Wiesmulluer and came within inches of snuffing me. Yes, sir, these boys could shoot. Well, I figured if force wouldn't work, it was time to use brainpower. Now, I'll admit that I'm a little rusty in that department, but I figured I had a leg up on those two. A plan began to hatch in my noggin. If I could just draw them in closer . . .

It'd grown quiet again, so I let out a low groan, then a cough and some choking sounds. "Didya hear that?" Lester hissed. "I tol' you I nailed him."

"I reckon you did at that. It sure enough sounded like he croaked," Elmo agreed solemnly. "You go check it out. I'll cover you from here in case one of them's playing possum."

I screwed my eyes shut and ground my teeth, fighting the impulse to let out a string of cuss words. I needed both of them to come down. I opened my eyes, watching as Lester picked his way carefully over to me. He walked right up to where I lay, standing in front of my head. As he reached out and started to poke me with his rifle, I grabbed his booted ankles and jerked hard.

Lester fell, screaming as he lit flat on his keister. Scrambling across the ground, I grabbed the front of his shirt and took a swipe at his head with my pistol. I don't know what the barrel of my gun hit, but it wasn't his head. Or if it did clip him on the melon, it didn't shut him up. No, sir, he commenced to bellering like a hungry calf.

The crash of a rifle cut across his screams, and I cringed, expecting to feel the bullet tearing through my body. Instead, all I felt was Lester's screams ripping through my eardrums.

"Mercy me! I done been shot," he bellered.

"Lester! Are you all right?" I heard Elmo call, but I didn't have time to worry about him right then. Lester was flopping around like a catfish on a flat rock, and I was having a time just holding him on the ground. Somewhere in the tussle, I'd lost hold of my shooter, but I finally got a hold of Lester's greasy hair. With one hand wrapped around a handful of his hair, I managed to hold his head still. The rest of him, though, was going like a thrashing machine I saw over at Beaver Falls. Every time he kicked, his spurs dug into the back of my legs. Well, let me tell you, it didn't take long to get a bellyful of that. Once I got his head pinned down, I rared back and busted him in the chops. As my big fist clobbered him, he quit squirming and his whole body went limp as a dishrag.

As I lay on top of him, I glanced up at Elmo. I could see him standing up, trying to see what was going on. He raised his rifle and took a couple of steps toward me. "Lester, are you all right?" he called as I felt around on the ground for my gun. "Lester," he called again as my search became desperate. Any minute, he might decide to stop talking and start shooting.

I snuck a peek up at Elmo. He started to sight down his rifle, then stopped and raised his head, stared at me for a second, then looked down the barrel of his rifle again. Just when I thought he would shoot, a shadowy figure rose up off the ground behind him and jabbed a pistol into Elmo's gizzard. Elmo dropped his rifle like it was red-hot and threw his hands into the air, his fingers clutching at the stars. "For Pete's sake, don't shoot!" he bawled.

The man behind him kicked the rifle away, then called down to me, "It's okay, Teddy. I got him!" I groaned and rolled on my back, throwing my arms wide. I knew that voice and to tell the truth, I'd just about soon be shot. "Teddy, are you all right, boy?"

"Yeah, Turley, I'm fine," I said tiredly. Cursing my luck, I climbed to my feet. With a start, I remembered Karl. A pang of guilt stabbing me, I rushed over to his side. I expected to find him dead, but I was in for a fooling; he was still breathing. Let me tell you, that was one tough old man.

"Turley, get over here," I cried out, and wrung my

hands. I didn't know nothing about taking care of a wounded man. I just hoped Turley did. "Turley, hurry up. Wiesmulluer's been shot!" I shouted, hoping to put some geddyup in the old trapper's getalong.

Not that it did a lot of good. Turley ambled along, stopping beside me. He pointed at the ground with his pistol. "You sit there and don't move," he told Elmo. As Elmo plopped to the ground, Turley sat his pistol on the ground and knelt beside Wiesmulluer. "Teddy, round up some wood and start a fire," Turley ordered in clipped tones.

I didn't move. I stood rooted to the spot. "Is he going to be all right?" I asked.

"I don't know. I need some light to see what I'm doing. Now get some wood and get me a fire going."

As I moved to do Turley's bidding, Elmo made a grab at Turley's pistol. Without turning a hair, Turley swung his fist backward, clouting Elmo right above the eyes. Elmo flopped over backward, yowling like a coon dog. "Shut up!" Turley barked. "You try that again, and I'll really give you something to howl about."

Figuring Turley had things well in hand, I went about my task. By the time I got the fire going, Turley had Wiesmulluer's shirt open and was hunched over the wound. "How's it look?" I asked, shifting my feet.

"I've seen worse," Turley grunted. "Go fetch my horse. I got some stuff in the saddlebags I'm going to need," Turley ordered, and pointed off to the south.

Following the direction of his pointing arm, I took

off in a pounding trot. It didn't take me but just a few minutes to find his horse and lead him back to the fire. "Give me the bags," Turley said, holding out his hand.

Without bothering to untie the strings, I ripped the bags loose from the saddle and passed them to Turley. As he pawed through the bags, I jammed my hands into my pockets and shuffled my feet in the dust. "What can I do to help?" I asked, and believe me, I felt about as useful as perfume on a pig.

"Here," Turley grunted and tossed me a ball of rawhide cord. "You can tie up those two before they cause any more trouble."

I gratefully set about the task, just danged glad that I didn't have to help with the doctoring. I reckon I'm a little squeamish when it comes to slopping around in a body's innards. Besides, I tend to be a mite heavy-handed. I'd likely kill him just trying to help. Yes, sir, I reckon hammering and swearing is more up my alley.

Now, I may not have the first clue what to do with a wounded man, but I sure knew how to handle a couple of dim-witted thugs like Lester and Elmo. Elmo was sitting up, rubbing his forehead. I didn't bother with any nice words, I just snatched him up by the scruff of his neck and plopped him down facefirst into the ground. I ground my knee into the small of his back and jerked his arms behind him. "Ouch!" Elmo howled, wiggling on the ground. "Watch it, you big lug!" he brayed. Spitting dirt from his mouth, he twisted his head around to look at me. "I shot you.

How come you ain't dead?'' he asked, wonder in his voice.

"You didn't shoot me; you shot him," I said and motioned my head in Wiesmulluer's direction.

"I did?" Elmo said, arching his eyebrows. "Huh? Well, I meant to shoot you." Elmo didn't say anything more. Well, nothing I could understand anyway. He sure did a lot of grumbling and mumbling under his breath. Finished tying him, I stood up. Elmo grunted and flopped around on the ground, then finally managed to roll onto his back. "You's the one they's paying to kill, ain't you?"

"That's what they tell me," I answered gruffly. I started to turn away, then stopped dead in my tracks. "Who's paying the money?" I asked, trying to keep a poker face.

"How the devil should I know that? We just heard about it. That's all," Elmo said, growling.

"If you don't know who was paying the money, how was you figuring on collecting it?" I countered, sure that I had him boxed in.

A stupefied look crossed his face, and he cocked his head off to one side as he thought it over. He scrunched up his eyebrows, and his face turned red from the effort. "You know, we never thought about that," he admitted wryly. "We just figured to drive off some cattle so you'd chase after us. Then we figured to catch you and kill you."

"What woulda you done if I hadn't chased after you?" I asked smugly.

Elmo's face beamed as a watermelon-eatin' grin

busted across his lips. "Now, that there is the beauty of my plan," he said and gave me a broad wink. "If you didn't chase after us, we figured to just drive the cows down south and sell them. Then we'd come back and get some more. Sooner or later, you was bound to follow us. Pretty smart, eh?"

"Oh yeah, real smart," I said sarcastically, and I started to tie Lester's hands. Lester groaned and struggled weakly, but I paid that no mind.

"Yep, I'm the brains of the outfit," Elmo allowed, puffing out his chest and smacking his lips. "My brother there, he's dumber than a box of rocks. Yes, sir, I'm the sharp one. Why, I had nigh on three months of regular schoolin'."

"Who you calling dumb?" Lester demanded, fighting wildly as I tried to tie him. "You take that back!" he screamed and fought to kick his brother.

Now, I'd just about had my fill of both of them. I was sorely tempted to wallop them over the head again. It didn't quite come to that. A little elbow grease and a lot of cussing seen me through the job.

"I been shot! Ain't you gonna tend to me?" Lester bawled.

"You ain't bleeding, so I don't reckon you're hurt too bad," I said and piled him down beside his brother, then went to find our horses.

By the time I gathered up Karl's horse and mine and returned to the fire, Turley was through working on Wiesmulluer and sat beside the fire, smoking a nasty-smelling pipe. "Is he going to live?" I asked.

Turley pulled the pipe from his mouth and shrugged

his shoulders as he studied it. ''Well, now, I don't rightly know,'' he admitted and began to tamp more tobacco into his pipe. ''A week is what we need,'' he said calmly.

''A week?'' I echoed, not at all sure what he meant.

''Yep. If he's up and around in a week, I'd say he will be fine. On the other hand, if he's stiff as a board and starting to smell a mite . . .''

It took a second for Turley's words to soak in, but when they did, my temper shot through the roof. ''Turley!'' I shouted, so mad that I sputtered, trying to find the words I wanted. And believe me, most of them that were coming to mind were not of the decent kind. I mean, while old man Wiesmulluer wasn't my favorite person, far from it in fact, I still didn't think it was hardly proper to be making jokes with him all stretched out on the ground.

As I was all set to launch into my tirade, Turley smiled and held up his hand. ''Save your breath to cool your porridge. I know what you are going to say.'' Turley took a big hit off his pipe and shook his head. ''Look, Teddy, I've done all I can. 'Bout all we can do now is wait and see what happens.''

With that, Turley spread out his blankets and promptly went to sleep. He went right to sleep, but I couldn't—not with Wiesmulluer lying there, maybe dying. 'Course, Elmo and Lester's bickering didn't help, and neither did Turley's snoring. I swear, for a dried-up, scrawny codger, he snored like a fat bear. A deaf man couldn't have slept through that. I spent the night sitting on the ground and worrying.

The morning sun found me in an evil mood. I was covered with bumps and bruises from last night's fighting, to say nothing of the backs of my legs. Lester's spurs had raked them raw as a north wind. Then of course there was my backside, which was cold and numb from spending the night sitting on the cold ground. All in all, I felt plumb miserable.

I reached out with the toe of my boot and prodded Turley none too gently. "Wake up," I said with a rumble.

Turley threw off his blankets, smiling sleepily. "You look terrible," he said, his voice practically bubbling. "I sure hope our patient is doing better than you."

With me tagging along, he crossed to where Wiesmulluer lay on the ground. To my surprise the old man was wide awake. "How are you feeling?" I asked softly.

Well, there was sure nothing soft about Wiesmulluer's reply. "Never mind that!" he roared, and struggled to sit up. "Did you find my cows?" he asked, finally getting up.

"Not yet," I answered nervously.

I moved in to try and help support him, but the old man slapped my hands away. "How come you never rounded up my cows?"

I leaned back and exchanged a glance with Turley, who turned away a smile on his leathery face. "Well, it was dark. Besides, we had to fix you up," I said. "We caught the guys that drove them off. We can go get your cows anytime."

"Well, you got time now. Go find my cows!"

I was ready to jump to it when Turley busted out laughing. "Boy, I sure must be one jim-dandy doctor. He sounds good as new to me," Turley howled, slapping his knee. But he turned serious as he looked down at Wiesmulluer. "You jest forget about them cows. Like Teddy said, we got the men that took them. I reckon them cows will be all right."

Wiesmulluer flinched, then looked over at Lester and Elmo. "Is that them?" he asked, and I nodded. "Which one of them shot me?" he demanded fiercely.

Both Elmo and Lester gulped and shrank away from Wiesmulluer's vicious glare. Lester recovered his voice first. "It wasn't me. It was Elmo!" he bawled.

"Says who? I shot at the big lug!" Elmo declared.

"Well, you missed him, 'cause you sure 'nough drilled the old geezer," Lester shouted and kicked his brother.

Wiesmulluer groaned and cussed under his breath as he flopped back down. "Aw, crud, do me a favor and just shoot them both."

Their eyes popping wide open, both brothers' heads snapped up so fast you could hear their necks crack. "Hey, hey. You cain't do that," Elmo blustered, a quiver in his voice.

"No, but we can take you into Whiskey City and toss you in jail," I said tiredly, then pulled Turley off to one side. "What about Wiesmulluer? Can he travel back to town?"

Turley chuckled, looking at me with a twinkle in his watery old eyes. "What's the matter, you already missing that little filly? Or maybe you don't trust ol' doc Turley to keep Wiesmulluer alive and breathing fire?''

''No,'' I lied on both counts. ''I just have things to tend to.''

''Yeah, I reckon,'' Turley agreed. He grinned, giving me a funny look. ''This ain't a good place for you to be hanging around. If them guys had been Nick Oakley, I reckon you'd be six feet under right now. As it was, them two came mighty near to doing the job themselves.''

''Yeah, and I guess I owe you. If you hadn't showed up when you did, things might have got a bit sticky,'' I mumbled, then swallowed hard and forced myself to say it. ''Thanks, Turley. You saved my bacon.''

Turley shrugged and clapped me on the back. ''Yes, sir, I reckon I did.''

''How did you find us? You didn't just happen along?''

''No, sir, I didn't,'' Turley agreed solemnly. ''Eddy tol' me what you was up to, and I figured ol' Turley best tag along and make sure you didn't get into any trouble. Didn't you ever stop to think that this is just the kind of trap someone like Oakley might set?''

''No, I didn't!'' I replied grumpily. I reckon I wasn't as good of a sheriff as I thought. 'Course, I hadn't been on the job all that long. The town just made me sheriff because I needed a job after I went broke ranching. I know, they'd felt sorry for me. Still, I didn't need Turley pointing out every tiny mistake I made. I'd just about took all of Turley's attitude that

I meant to. I mean, I'd said thank you, and that was all I wanted to hear on the subject. "What about Wiesmulluer? Can we move him?"

Turley shrugged. "Sure, if he thinks he feels up to it."

Well, that old man was more than ready to move. So with him on a litter and Lester and Elmo tied in their saddles, we set out for town. We made miserable time, having to go slow and stop often so Wiesmulluer could rest.

Night caught us still several miles from Whiskey City. I dearly wanted to push on, but because of Wiesmulluer's condition, I called a halt and we made camp.

The next day about midmorning, we rode up to Whiskey City. As the town came into view, I jerked my horse to a stop. "What's the matter?" Turley asked, spurring his horse up beside me.

"Something's wrong," I said, trying to decide what it was. "The place looks deserted," I said slowly. "It looks like a ghost town."

It was true not a soul stirred, and not so much as one horse stood at the hitching rails. At this time of day, there should be someone moving around. Then I saw it, the body lying in the middle of the street.

Chapter Five

The moment I saw the body lying in the middle of the street, I slapped the spurs to my horse and we took off like a bullet. As I pounded into town, Turley Simmons rode right at my side. By then, I could see that the man lying in the street was none other than Cimarron Bob.

Before my horse could skid to a stop, I jumped to the ground, drawing my pistol as my boots thudded against the ground. Pistol in hand, I spun around, raking the town with my eyes. I didn't find any attackers, nor did I see any bullet holes or other signs that there had been an attack. "What the devil?" I muttered, turning to look at the fallen Cimarron Bob.

His back creaking like an outhouse door and a mad expression on his face, Cimarron Bob sat up. He waved his hand in front of his face, coughing and sputtering on the dirt we'd kicked up. "What do you think you are doing, you big mullet head?" he growled.

"Huh?" I grunted, lowering my gun slowly. "We thought there had been an attack on the town."

Cimarron Bob cursed, Turley cackled, and I moaned, knowing this meant misery for me. "What made you think that?" Cimarron Bob growled.

I planted my big feet in the middle of the road, starting to get real mad. "We thought you had been shot. You were lying in the middle of the street." I stopped and scratched my head. "Why were you lying in the middle of the street?"

Cimarron Bob gave me a long stare, his eyes cutting into me like a hay sickle. "Well, if it's any of your business, I've decided to die today. I was trying to go peacefully and with some respect, when you fools came charging in."

"How come you decided to lay down and die in the middle of the street?"

"I didn't want to die where nobody would find me until I started to stink," he answered, like that explained everything.

"Well, move out of the middle of the street. Somebody's liable to run over you," I grumbled as Turley laughed. "What's so funny?"

Turley cackled and pointed in the direction from which we came. "Your prisoners, all I can see of them is their backsides going over the hill."

I swore quickly, seeing he was right. Lester and Elmo were going over the hill like the devil himself was chasing them. I started to chase after them. Then, with a start, I remembered old man Wiesmulluer, who we'd just left lying out there.

Groaning and pounding my thigh, I sprinted for my horse. Long before I reached Wiesmulluer's litter, I could tell from the grunts and roars coming from the litter that the old man wasn't happy with me.

I packed Wiesmulluer into town. For a man who'd taken a bullet in the gizzard, he sure had a lot of wind-power. He wasn't happy that we'd deserted him, and he sure wasn't happy that Lester and Elmo got away. Yes, sir, he gave my ears a right good blistering, but by the time we reached the hotel, he was wearing down. Not that I got a moment's peace. Oh, no. We bumped into Eddy. She saw me carrying the old man into the hotel and went nuts.

Now, Eddy ain't the type of woman to keel over in a faint or burst out in hysterics. Naw, she didn't do anything like that. She just got mad. I mean, she took charge of things and helped me get her pa into the hotel. She was a big help, but the whole time, I could see her kettle was boiling.

As soon as we got him stuffed into a bed, she drug me out into the hall. As she pulled me out the door, I shot a pleading look at Wiesmulluer. For a man that'd been shooting his mouth off earlier, he sure turned meek and quiet now. I reckon he knew as well as me what was coming and wanted no part of it.

I didn't have to wait long. Eddy pulled the door shut, then stepped back and crossed her arms. "What happened?" she asked, tapping her foot like a woodpecker.

"We was ambushed," I answered, unable to meet her gaze.

Her foot went from tapping to stomping. "I told you it was foolish to go off chasing after those outlaws by yourselves. I told you to wait for help."

"I wanted to wait. It was your pop that wanted to go," I reminded her. 'Course, for all the good it done me, I might as well have been talking to a tree stump. That woman heard only what she wanted to.

She put her hands on her hips. "You're supposed to be a lawman. Can't you catch a couple of cattle rustlers without getting my father shot?"

"They weren't just rustlers; they were killers out to collect that bounty on my head. Besides, we caught them," I informed her.

Her foot froze in midtap and her eyebrows shot up. "Where are they now?"

Dad-gummed nosy woman! Why did she always have to be so snoopy? I knew she wasn't going to quit hounding me until I gave her an answer, but I didn't want to. I shuffled my feet, jammed my hands down in my pockets, and looked at the floor. "Aw, all right, they got away," I mumbled. Then I got mad. "It weren't my fault! It was that old fool Cimarron Bob. When I saw him sprawled out in the middle of the street, I thought there had been a raid on the town. While I was checking it out, them outlaws scrammed."

When I finally managed to look her in the eye, I saw her features had softened. In fact, she wore an almost wistful expression. "He's such a strange old man," she murmured.

"He's crazy as an addled coon," I added.

Eddy laughed delightfully and patted my chest with her hand. "I feel sorry for him. It must be absolutely terrible to be so old and broken down that you can't do what you used to do."

"What he used to do was kill people!"

She laughed again, then raised up on her tiptoes and kissed my cheek. "Oh, don't be silly. All of that is just a lot of loose-mouthed talk by folks who should know better," she said, then gave me a stern look. "You be nice to him. He needs a friend right now."

Now, I had an altogether different idea about what that old coot needed, but I had the good sense to keep that under my hat. Instead of speaking my mind, I gave her a quick grin and a kiss. She patted my chest again, smiling up at me. "You run along while I tend to Daddy."

"Yeah, I reckon I best run out and tell your mother what happened," I decided.

Eddy stopped, her hand resting on the doorknob. "Don't go by yourself. Get Turley or somebody to go with you. Those men might try to come after you again."

"Yeah, yeah," I mumbled, turning and walking down the hall. "Dang woman, I don't know why everybody thinks I need a nursemaid. I can take care of myself," I mumbled under my breath as I walked down the hall.

"Teddy," Eddy said warningly. "You get someone to go with you."

I hunched my shoulders. I forgot that she could hear a pin drop a mile away. Before she could light into me, I ducked my head and scooted out of the place.

I trooped outside, gathering my horse and Wiesmulluer's. I didn't see Turley, but his horse was in front of the saloon. He was likely inside, telling anyone that would listen how he'd saved me.

Making a face at the saloon, I led the two horses down to the stable. Mr. Burdett looked up from his forge, a mad expression on his face. "Teddy, where the devil have you been? I've been working myself to death down here. Why, yesterday I went and jerked a muscle in my back. It's been paining me something terrible."

"I had sheriffing business to take care of," I replied surlily as I tied my horse.

Burdett snorted and rolled his eyes. "Well, are you here to work now?" he asked hopefully.

"Can't. I've got to ride out to the Wiesmulluer place. Karl's been shot."

"Shot? How'd he get shot?"

"Some rustlers ran off a bunch of his cattle. When we caught up with them, they put up a fight and he got shot. He's over at the hotel right now. Eddy's taking care of him."

"Are you going to be in to work tomorrow?"

I stared at him in disbelief. "Jeez, I just told you Wiesmulluer has been shot. Can't you forget about yourself for just a minute?"

"You said Eddy was taking care of him. It ain't like you can do anything for him," he said belligerently.

Ignoring him, I led Wiesmulluer's horse inside the barn and started stripping off the saddle. "Dang, boy, can't a man find a place in this whole blamed town where he can die in peace?" Cimarron Bob growled as he sat up behind a pile of feed.

"How about the jail?" I grumbled and slapped the saddle down on the fence. "I got half a mind to toss you in there for a few days just on general principles."

Cimarron Bob snorted and cursed under his breath. "I wish I could still hold a gun. I'd shoot you and have a high time spending the money."

"Well, you ain't up to the job, so just lie over there and keep quiet."

I finished the job and stomped out of the barn with Cimarron Bob's curses ringing in my ears. Burdett shot me a hard glance, but I paid him no mind as I swung aboard my horse and rode out of town.

I arrived at the Wiesmulluer place just shortly after dark. Now, I fully intended to spend the night, then escort Marie back into town the next morning, but she would have none of that. Before I could hardly explain what had happened, she was throwing stuff into a bag and shoving me out to the barn to saddle her a horse.

"It's dark out there, and it's a long trip. Wouldn't you be more comfortable in a wagon?" I protested.

Marie stopped throwing stuff in the bag long enough to throw a hard frown in my direction. "A wagon would take too long. Saddle me a horse and get a fresh one for yourself.''

''Yes, ma'am,'' I replied and hurried out to the barn. I snagged two horses from the corral and led them inside. By the time I had my saddle on one and Marie's on the other, she was waiting on me. She waited on the porch, perched on top of a mountain of baggage. ''Teddy, would you load my bags?''

My mouth dropped open as I looked at the bags. I seen folks cross the prairie and not take along that much stuff. I don't reckon them horses liked it much neither. I swear, I could hear their backs groan and see their knees buckle a mite as I piled them bags on their backs. ''Is there anything left in the house?'' I grumbled.

Marie stomped her foot and gave me a flashing look I knew very well. That look reminded me so much of Eddy that I staggered back a step, the hair on the back of my neck rising. ''Are you going to stand there with your mouth hanging open or finish loading the bags?'' Marie demanded.

''Sorry, ma'am,'' I mumbled, hurriedly tossing the rest of the bags on the horse and lashing them in place. ''Don't you think we should run by Bobby and Betsy's place and tell them what's happened?''

''No,'' Marie said, shaking her head as she bustled over to her horse. ''Betsy is supposed to come over in the morning. We was going to do some canning. I left her a note.''

Now, I wasn't sure that a note was the best way to break such news, but I didn't argue. I'd learned long ago that arguing with the women in the Wiesmulluer family was like banging your head against a barrel cactus.

With the moonlight to guide us, we set out for town. We didn't ride three miles before my head began to nod and my eyes grew heavy. I tried to spark up a conversation just to keep awake, but Marie didn't seem of a mind to talk. So we rode in silence, the stillness broken only by my occasional yawn. I was just about to fall from the saddle when we heard the cry in the night.

I shot a quick glance at Marie. ''That sounded like somebody hurt real bad,'' I whispered and slid my pistol from the holster.

''It came from over there,'' Marie whispered, pointing off to the left.

My eyes followed her pointing finger, but I couldn't see anything. I didn't trust the situation. In my mind, I could still see the bullet that whipped out of the night and smashed Wiesmulluer to the ground.

''Stay here,'' I whispered as I slid off my horse, trying to move quiet as possible.

''I'm coming with you,'' Marie said, determination in her hushed voice.

Scowling, I motioned frantically for her to stay. My eyes trained on the spot from where the noise came, I dropped my pistol into the holster and eased my rifle from the saddle boot. Carrying the rifle in both hands ready to fire if the need arose, I moved out. I moved slowly, trying to blend in with the shadows.

I couldn't see much, so I tried to concentrate on my

hearing. I heard the sound of hoarse breathing, sounding like someone was choking on their last breath. I paused, sweeping the whole area with my eyes.

It came to me that a man pretending to be hurt would make a perfect ambush. Squatting low, I circled carefully around the coughing sounds. As I paused to catch my breath, the shadow of a man flitted in front of me. The man took cover behind a tree. He hugged up next to the tree and peered intently into the darkness.

Moving my head slow and easy, I looked in the same direction. At first I didn't see it, but then it moved and I saw the body lying on the ground. As my eyes strained to see through the gloom, I realized, the body on the ground was a woman!

A fit of rage swept over me and I leaped off the ground. I grabbed the man behind the tree by the scruff of the neck. With one hand, I lifted the man plumb off the ground and slammed him up against the tree. I jabbed my rifle viciously into the pit of his stomach and felt a grim satisfaction as he grunted in pain.

"Teddy, help!" I heard Marie Wiesmulluer scream, the fear in her voice sending a shiver up my spine.

Grinding the rifle into my captive's belly, I looked over my shoulder, trying to locate Marie. I couldn't see her, but I heard the cold, jeering voice that rang out from the dark. "Hey, sheriff man. Toss down your guns. Unless you want to start digging a grave for this nice lady!"

Chapter Six

All of a sudden my muscles went limp, and I let the rifle fall to my side. My former captive jumped away from the tree and snatched the weapon out of my suddenly numb hands. In a wink, he reversed the weapon and drove the butt into my belly.

Gasping in pain, I doubled over, only vaguely aware that the man jerked my pistol from my holster. "Lester, Lester, I got him!" he shouted, then commenced to proddin' me with that rifle. "Get over there," he grunted, and pushed me in the direction of the woman on the ground.

As we drew closer, I could see the woman was tied and gagged, her bound hands lashed to a thick stake driven into the ground. What's more, I could see who it was, and the sight of her face made my jaw go slack and my whole body tremble. Iris Winkler!

Now, from the beginning, I'd had an inkling that Lester and Elmo weren't the sharpest two jaspers around, but this was sheer stupidity, even for them. That woman made a rabid wolf seem like a gentle lapdog. Ticking her off was like smoking in a powder room; sooner or later it was gonna blow up on you. If Iris ever got loose, she'd rip those boys to shreds.

"Quit your gawking and start a fire," Elmo barked and gave me another shove.

While I put the fire together, Lester and Marie came up to the camp. Marie led our horses while Lester followed, keeping her covered. "Elmo, you should see all the bags they got tied on these horses. I tell you, we hit the mother lode this time!" Lester cried.

Elmo licked his lips, staring at all the bags. "Doggy," he whispered slowly.

A pumpkin-eatin' grin on his face, Lester jumped up and down, dancing a little jig. "What you suppose is in them bags, huh? Gold, maybe?" he asked, his grin getting so wide I figured his eyes would pop out of his head.

Elmo whipped my rifle around, pointing it at Marie. "OK, lady, what you got in them packs?"

Her hands on hips, Marie branded the scrawny Elmo with a fiery stare. "All that's in them bags is clothes and some personal items," she answered quietly.

"You expect me to believe that?" Elmo demanded, stepping up jaw-to-jaw with Marie. "Lester, look through them packs," he ordered, and while Lester pawed through the bags, Elmo and Marie stared each other down.

"No wolfin', Elmo. All they got here is a bunch of clothes and women's foofaraw," Lester called out.

Elmo made a face at Marie. Then all of a sudden, he leaned back, a leering grin on his face. "Well, well, what do we have here?" he sneered.

"What? What?" Lester screamed, jumping up and down.

"Don't you see? These two was runnin' off together," Elmo replied knowingly.

I groaned and shook my head. I swear, if brains were rainwater, these two wouldn't have enough between them to make a puddle in the bottom of a thimble.

Lester's ragged teeth showed as he flashed me a sly grin. "Like older women, do you?" he asked, digging an elbow into my side and winking broadly.

I groaned again and slapped the side of my face. If there was any way in the world to get things wrong, trust these two to do it. If it weren't for the seriousness of the situation, this would almost be funny. Marie Wiesmulluer sure never saw the humor in it. She stomped her foot and like to snapped their heads off. "Listen, adobe brain, Teddy and I are not running off together. He's engaged to my daughter, for heaven's sake."

"Yeah, sure," Elmo agreed, but he snickered under his breath and rolled his eyes toward the sky. He leered at Marie, then nodded at me. "You old dog, you," he said and punched my arm.

Marie wiped that sly smile off his face with a swipe of her hand. He staggered back, braying like a barnyard donkey as Marie whacked him across the head. "You stupid fool," she said in a blistering tone. She drew herself up to her full height, looking down her nose at Elmo. "My husband has been shot. Teddy is escorting me into town so I can be with him."

"No wolfin'?" Lester asked, scratching his head. "Say, you ain't married to that crusty old geezer that Elmo plugged?"

The thunderstorm that flashed in Marie's eyes was wicked enough to put a rattlesnake hunting his hole. I know she sure backed Elmo up a couple of steps. He grinned sickly and held his hands up in front of his face. "Look, ma'am, I sure never meant to pop your husband. I was aiming to dust that big gorilla there," he said, jerking his head at me.

I don't know if she even heard him. She was screaming some very definite references to his ancestry. With a last insult, she sprang at Elmo, her hands clawing at his grizzled face like eagle talons.

With a bleat of pure terror, Elmo went to backpedaling, his legs moving like a man treading water. Seeing a chance, I lunged at Lester, who was engrossed in watching the scrap. If Marie could just keep Elmo busy long enough for me to take care of Lester, we just might escape these bozos. The only problem was that Elmo didn't have the guts to stand toe-to-toe with Marie. Squealing like a mashed pig, he turned and fled. 'Course, like everything else, he couldn't even do that right. He managed to tangle his spurs and fall.

Too late, I saw him tumble into my path. I tried to veer away, but I'm a mighty big man once I get to rumbling, I'm pretty much locked into a straight-line course. Well, to make a long story short, that danged Elmo crashed into my knees. Losing my balance, I staggered forward, smacking headfirst into a tree. A bolt of lightning shot down my neck and spine, curling my toes. Even my teeth were smarting as I wobbled on shaky legs, my head feeling like I'd just been stuck headfirst into a snowbank. All of a sudden, my legs buckled and I lit flat on my backside. Then everything went sorta black.

When I woke up, my hands were tied in front of me. A still-seething Marie sat beside me while Lester tied her hands. Elmo stood back, covering us with a rifle. The rifle in his hands was shaking, and I noticed that his face was scratched and clawed like he just went ten rounds with a catamount. "You got her tied up yet?" he asked, his voice quavering to match his hands.

"You can relax now," Lester hooted, slapping his knee as he stepped back. "Boy, she sure worked you over!"

"Aw, shut up," Elmo growled and kicked the dirt. "She surprised me. That's all."

"I reckon she done more than that. You should see your face," Lester said, snickering. Still chuckling, he walked over to where Iris was tied. Now, while we'd been fighting, Iris had been working to get free. She'd dang near wore a hole in the ground from thrashing against her bonds.

Poor Lester, he didn't have a clue what he was getting into. He cut Iris loose from the stake and dumped her beside Marie. He pulled the gag from her mouth, then staggered back under the onslaught of her words. The way she tied into him, I bet he thought he'd just uncapped a volcano. She called him every dirty name under the sun. Why, she even came up with a few I'd never heard before. His eyes wide, Lester hurriedly stuffed the gag back into her mouth, cutting her off in midcuss.

"Lordy, I'd hate to meet her in a back alley," Elmo muttered.

"I'd say so, since the nice one done whupped you," Lester howled, pointing to the scratches on Elmo's face. As he stopped laughing, he looked at the two women. "What are we gonna do with them?"

Elmo drew himself up to his full height, puffing out his scrawny chest as he rubbed his chin. "Well now, I've been thinking on that. I think we should hold them for ransom."

Lester frowned and spat on the ground. "I dunno," he muttered, digging a finger in his ear. "Who'd pay to get that old bat back?" he asked, then yelped as Iris kicked him in the shin.

"Well, maybe not her, but I bet that old coot that I shot would pay a pile to get his woman back," Elmo said, then grinned at his brother. "Who knows, maybe they would pay us to keep the old battle-ax?"

"That would take a lot of money. I don't like her," Lester replied.

"Never mind that now. First thing we have to do

is dust ol' tree stump there,'' Elmo said, gesturing to me.

"Well, drill him and let's go collect the money," Lester urged.

"You want me to shoot him?" Elmo asked, pulling at the seat of his britches. "I figured you'd want to do it."

"Ah . . . well, I'd do it, but I spranged my trigger finger the other day," Lester mumbled.

"How in the world could you sprain a finger?" Elmo demanded, and to tell the truth I wanted to hear the answer to that one myself.

"Well, the other day, I was picking my nose and my fool horse rared up and bumped my elbow. Wrenched my finger something awful it did."

"Well, don't you know better than to use your trigger finger to pick your nose?" Elmo growled disgustedly.

"Well, yeah sure, I know that now, but I didn't know it then."

Now, how in the world can you argue with that? I couldn't, and I reckon Elmo couldn't neither 'cause he just stood there, his mouth hanging open and looking like he'd just been run over by a herd of turtles. "Well, all right, I reckon I can do the job," Elmo replied finally.

He took his rifle and stepped directly in front of me. He checked the rifle, then licked the front sight. He popped his finger in his mouth, then held it up, testing the wind. He leaned the rifle against his leg, then spat in his hands and rubbed them together. Finally ready, he picked up the rifle and pointed it right at me.

Now, it hadn't really dawned on me that they actually meant to kill me. I'd been laughing at their antics, but when he steered that rifle my way, the laughter died and a knot sprang in my throat. I tried to swallow, but couldn't. I dearly wanted to look away, but my eyes were glued on that rifle. They widened as I saw Elmo's finger tighten on the trigger. My whole body jumped, and my heart almost stopped dead when I heard that rifle boom.

Chapter Seven

I didn't feel the hot flash of pain like I thought I would. In fact, the only pain I felt was in my eardrums from Marie's screams. I tensed my muscles against the pain I knew would come. "You missed!" I heard Lester bellow, and I blew out the breath I'd been holding in.

"You shoot like a sheep farmer!" Lester howled. "Why, you missed by a good four feet."

"The sun was in my eyes," Elmo shot back angrily.

"Sun?" Lester screeched, waving his arms at the sky. "It's nighttime."

That kinda set Elmo back on his heels, but not for long. "Well, I was afraid of hitting one of them women. If we are going to ransom them, we don't want them all shot up."

"Say now, that's right good thinking," Lester said,

bobbing his head up and down like a man dunking for apples. He turned to me and pointed a finger at a tree on the other side of the fire. "You, lawman, move over there."

"No, I ain't gonna do it," I told him.

"You move or I'll move you," Lester threatened, but I just looked up at him, my jaw set firm. Lester swore under his breath, then grabbed the front of my shirt. He strained and grunted, but he didn't have enough moxie to get me off the ground. Cursing, he stepped back and looked at his partner. "Would you get over here and help me move this big lug?"

Looking awfully superior, Elmo shook his head slowly. "Lester, I swear, you don't have the brains of a firefly. Don't mess with him; move the women."

For a second, Lester looked plumb baffled, then his whole face lit up as the idea finally bored through his thick skull. "They's smaller, ain't they?"

Elmo nodded and leaned on his rifle, waiting while Lester drug Iris and Marie off to the side. They put up a scrap, but they were more the size Lester could handle. 'Course, if they hadn't have been tied, I reckon either one of them coulda took him. By the time he got them moved, poor Lester was sweating puddles big enough to fill a bathtub. "All right, there you go. Now plug the jasper," Lester said between gasps.

Elmo took up the rifle; it was my turn to sweat as he headed the dang thing my way. He squinted down the barrel for a long time. Once he stopped and licked his finger and wiped a smug of dirt off the barrel.

Satisfied that the gun was clean, he commenced to drawing a bead again.

"What are you waiting on? Shoot him," Lester bawled.

Elmo scowled and lowered the weapon. "Aw, now you went and done it. You busted my concentration," he complained. Elmo lifted the gun again, muttering under his breath. "I don't know how I'm supposed to shoot with you yakking in my ear." Still muttering, he drew aim, but didn't shoot. "Aw, I can't shoot with him staring at me with them hound-dog eyes. Make him stop lookin' at me," Elmo whined.

"Yeah sure, can do," Lester replied and strutted over to me. "Stop looking at him."

"No," I replied.

"I'm a-warning you," Lester said sternly. "Now, if you know what's good for you, you'll be a good sheriff and turn your head."

"No."

Lester leaned in close and gave me an exasperated look. "Now, you ain't being at all helpful." He took hold of my ears and turned my head, but as soon as he let go, I turned it back. "Stop that!" he screamed, jumping up and down. He twisted my head, but again I snapped it back. "You do that again and I'll shoot you myself," he thundered, his fingers tickling the butt of his gun.

"You got a hurt finger," I reminded him.

"Oh, yeah," Lester muttered, a crestfallen expression settling on his face. Slowly a crafty look pushed the defeated one off his horse face. "My finger may

be sore, but there ain't nothing wrong with my boots.
Now, you look away or I'll stomp you.''

He waited a long second, but when I didn't look
away, he spat on the ground, then hitched up his
britches. ''So, you want to do this the hard way. That's
fine by me.'' He jumped into the air, drawing both
feet up ready to stomp my legs, which stretched out
in front of me. Just before he came down, I jerked my
legs outta the way. He smacked the ground all out of
kilter, and I could tell the impact jarred him plumb up
to the roots of his hair. He hung on his feet for a
second, his whole body quivering like a wire fence in
a windstorm. Then his knees buckled and he lit flat on
his saddle cover.

He didn't stay down long; in a flash he was back
on his feet. He glared down at me, wiped his nose on
his sleeve, then went to stomping like a man trying to
make wine out of walnuts. Every time he'd stomp, I'd
slide my legs out of the way. Growling and cussing,
he kept at it. I swear, the front of my shirt was almost
soaked, he was spitting and frothing so much. Finally,
he gave up and flopped to the ground, panting like a
coon dog after a long run. ''Aw crud, Elmo, just shoot
the slop dog,'' he groaned.

Elmo scratched his chin and shook his head. ''I've
been standing here a-thinking,'' he said slowly. ''Just
up and shootin' him ain't gonna be easy as we fig-
gered. But I reckon we could hang him real easy.''

Right then I started to get scared again. As Elmo
and Lester found out, it ain't an easy thing to look a
man square in the eye and shoot him dead. Hanging,

now, that might be an altogether different proposition. 'Course, that would mean that Elmo actually came up with a good idea, so maybe the odds were in my favor.

Lester musta liked the idea, 'cause he jumped up off the ground and rushed over to my horse. Well, Wiesmulluer's actually, but I reckon that don't matter. Lester tore my saddle off, then led the beast under a tree. Like a monkey, he took my rope, then scurried up the tree. Leaning out, he tied the rope hard and fast to the limb that hung over my horse.

Elmo sauntered over to me, a smug expression riding on his face. "Okay, big boy, get up on that horse," he ordered, but I just stared up at him. "I'm warning you, redwood, get up on that horse 'fore I have to shoot you."

I smiled up at him. "Go ahead and shoot," I dared.

Elmo stared at me, his face turning beet red. He wiped his mouth quickly and looked around. With a quick jerk, he yanked his hat down, then snatched his pistol. His whole body trembling, he shook that gun in my face. "You best get up on that horse."

"No, I ain't doing it," I said flatly.

Elmo's face turned so red, I figured his whiskers would catch on fire. For a second, I thought I'd pushed him too far and he would shoot. Then, with an oath, he rammed that pistol back in his belt and turned away. "Lester, haul your scrawny backside over here and help me."

A pained expression on his face, Lester straightened up and ambled over to his brother. "Whatcha got in mind?" he asked, sounding wary as a wild wolf.

''If he won't climb up on that horse, we'll put him there.''

''Are you plumb loco? We'd never lift him. He weighs more than a team of plow horses.''

''Never mind that. Just help me,'' Elmo said, growling.

Together they managed to drag me to my feet, despite my best efforts to stay on the ground. I dug in my heels and done my best imitation of a mule, but they still managed to rassle me over to that horse. Together, they boosted me up off the ground, but when they tried to sling me across that horse's back, I put my feet against his flank and pushed hard. The extra weight buckled their knees and the lot of us crashed to the ground with me on top.

For a minute we had quite a tussle on the ground, but there were two of them and my hands were tied. The upshot of the whole deal was they managed to worm out from underneath me. Lester scrambled to his feet, glaring down at me. ''You done that a'purpose!'' he stuttered, pointing an accusing finger down at me. ''That weren't at all neighborly!'' he yelled and kicked me a couple of times in the short ribs.

Them kicks drove the wind clean outta my lungs and doubled me over. By the time I got some wind back in my kitchen, they had me slung over that horse and that rope around my neck.

His face red, Elmo stepped back and bent over to catch his breath. ''OK, Lester, slap that horse and let's get this over with.''

Lester frowned and rubbed the stubble on his chin. "I don't know if I can," he said slowly.

"Your sore finger ain't gonna keep you from slapping a horse," Elmo pointed out.

While they argued, I tried to reach behind my head and loosen the rope. With my hands tied together, I couldn't reach the slipknot behind my head. Giving up on that idea, I tried to lean forward and grab the horse's mane. If I could get ahold of his mane, maybe I could keep him from bolting. The problem was, I was perched plumb to the back of that horse, and the rope around my neck was tight. I just couldn't lean forward enough to catch the mane.

"Would you whack that horse!" I heard Elmo scream, his voice shrill with anger. His face set in stubborn lines and his arms folded across his chest, Lester shook his head. "Dang it, Lester, I have to do everything!" Elmo shouted and threw his hat on the ground.

Well, that did it. When Elmo threw his hat down, that fool horse took off like he thought he was some kind of racehorse. I made a wild desperate grab, but there wasn't anything to grab. A scream pouring out of my throat, I slid off the back of that horse. I hit the end of that rope with a painful snap.

Gagging and choking, my feet pedaling wildly, I dangled at the end of the rope, slowly growing weaker. Through the roaring in my ears, I could hear Elmo and Lester celebrating, thinking they were about to collect the ten grand on my head. And right then, I believed it myself.

With the last bit of my strength, I reached over my head and grabbed the rope. With a surge, I pulled myself, but the knot around my neck didn't loosen. I hung on as long as I could, but my strength was gone and I had to let go. I hit the end of the rope with a jarring thud and a red mist filled my vision, as the sound of Elmo and Lester's voice drifted away until I couldn't hear them anymore.

Chapter Eight

When I hit the bottom of the rope it twanged like a guitar string and danged near jerked my head clean off. Right on the heels of that twang, I heard a crack that sounded like a rifle shot. The next thing I knew, my boots hit the dirt. My legs weren't ready to take my weight and they buckled, my knee whacking me in the chin.

As I rolled on the ground, I saw Elmo stretched out cold as a wedge. Beside him was the tree branch with rope still tied around it.

I tore that rope from around my neck and sucked in deep mouthfuls of the clean fresh air. Lester stood across from me, his mouth sagging down to his belt buckle as he stared blindly at his brother. He turned his head slowly, his eyes bugging out. "You kilt him!"

"Oh, I did not," I said tiredly. "He's moving."

"Oh, yeah," Lester conceded as Elmo tried to get up. "Well, it still weren't a nice thing to do, hitting him in the head thataway. My mammy always told me to treat folks nice."

"You were trying to kill me!" I screamed.

Lester gave me a look like a parent trying to explain something to a kid. "Well, yeah, sure we was, but we were being nice about it. I mean, we coulda just gut shot you and let you bleed to death."

I groaned and collapsed back to the ground. Right about then, I was ready to shoot myself. At least I wouldn't have to listen to the same loose-mouthed tough talk over and over.

While them two had been busy trying to string me up, Marie had been working on the knots that held Iris. Well, she somehow got Iris free and the old bat came off the ground like a scalded dog.

Now, most folks woulda cut and run, but not ol' Iris. She lit into them boys like a lumberjack into a redwood. What I mean to say is that she hiked up her skirts and booted Elmo in the ribs. Now Iris wasn't the type to tiptoe around in some prissy, frilly slippers. No, siree Bob, she had on a pair of full-grown stompers. When she planted them alongside Elmo's ribs, he gave a little hop and grunted like a pig in the mud.

I reckon if she had enough time, she likely woulda caved his whole side in, but Lester jumped in the air, screeching and waving his shooter like a man painting a fence. "Stop that, you old biddy!" he shouted, froth flying out of his mouth. "I swear, I'll blast the whole lot of you."

I reckon he convinced Iris, 'cause she backed away like a wary wolf. When Elmo finally regained his senses, he and Lester spent a whole hour screeching and screaming at each other as they tried to figure out their next move. After all that, the best they could come up with was to sleep on it and decide something in the morning. They tied Marie, Iris, and me to a tree, then went to sleep.

As the others slept, I sat with my back against the tree, my mind running flat out. I kept toying with the idea of making a break for it. The two brothers had already shown that they couldn't just up and shoot me. 'Course, if they saw me running away, they might just lose their heads and blast me. Still, I decided to keep my eyes open for the chance.

Long in there, I sorta drifted off to dreamland. When I awoke the sun was just waking up itself. The two brothers were still sleeping, so I made a pass at getting the ropes loose. It weren't no use. They musta used ten miles of rope. Giving up on that, I settled down to wait until they woke up. And that took awhile.

I always thought them mountain boys were early risers, but not these two. I swear, they could sleep the hair off a bear.

When they finally did get up, they staggered around the camp, yawning, snorting, and grunting. "Get a fire going and get us some breakfast," Elmo ordered, stretching his scrawny arms to the sky.

Lester grumbled as he worked, but he did manage to get a fire burning. "I don't know why I have to do all the work," he mumbled. "I mean, it ain't like your arms is broke. You could . . ." All of a sudden, Lester's face broke into a sly grin. "Say, why do I have to do all the cooking? We got them two women over there."

Iris snorted and dug her heels in the dirt. "If you think I'm going to cook for you, you got another thing coming," she said, sniffing and glaring at them. "It'd be a cold day in—"

"Shut up, you old biddy," Lester barked and shook the gag in her face. "I wasn't talking to you anyways. I was talking about her," he said and pointed a bony finger at Marie.

"No way!" Elmo screeched, his fingers stealing to the scratches on his face. "We ain't letting her loose. She's a wildcat!"

"Well, if you want something to eat, you're gonna have to cut her loose or do it yourself, 'cause I ain't gonna."

"All right, let her loose, but you keep an eye on her and keep her away from me. I'm going to fetch the horses."

Lester didn't waste no time. He scuttled over to us and started sawing Marie loose. "Who said I would agree to cook for you?" Marie asked.

Lester stopped cutting and whipped his hat off, mashing it into a ball. "Please, ma'am," he pleaded, looking at Marie with wide eyes. "I'm powerful hungry. Why, I bet you folks are a mite peaked yourselves.'' He turned real serious, leaning in to whisper. ''Take it from me, ma'am, you don't want to eat Elmo's cooking.''

''Bad?'' Marie asked, matching his deadly tone.

Lester made a face like a man who'd just taken a hit off a vinegar bottle. ''Powerful bad, ma'am. Killed the best dog we ever had, his vittles did.''

''A dog?'' Marie asked, a smile playing on her lips.

''Yep,'' Lester answered. ''Two hogs and a billy goat too.''

He shook his head sadly. ''You know, I always liked that dog. I'd sure hate for something like that to happen to you.''

Marie laughed and held up her hands in mock defense. ''OK, OK. I'll cook for you.''

A smile busted across Lester's face as he jumped to his feet and kicked his heels together. ''Jim dandy!'' he yelled, rubbing his hands together and smacking his lips.

''Oh, Lester, there is one thing,'' Marie said, and the look of joy washed off Lester's face. ''If I'm going to cook, you'll have to finish untying me,'' Marie said sweetly.

Lester's shoulders sagged and he blew out a big sigh. ''Whew, that was a close one,'' he said, looking over at me.

''Well, I never!'' Iris sniffed, glaring at Marie. ''Marie Wiesmulluer, I simply cannot believe that you are going to cook for these two hooligans.''

''Danged old biddy,'' I heard Lester mumble under his breath. I had to smile. I'd muttered them same words a time or two my ownself. Lester finally cut Marie free and climbed to his feet. His face bursting with righteous indignation, he straightened his clothes, then glared down at Iris. "You jest keep your trap shut, else you won't get no grub!" he threatened.

He turned and followed Marie to the fire, but I could still hear him mumbling and grumbling. "Danged old bat. Too bad there ain't a price on her pointy head." He pulled out his pistol and tried twirling it on the end of his finger, promptly dropping the weapon in the dirt. "I wouldn't have any trouble blasting her," he griped as he picked up the hogleg and rammed it back in the holster.

As Marie piled grub into the skillet, cooking and stirring, Elmo trotted the horse up to the camp. He had the animals saddled and ready. Lester pried his eyes away from the skillet long enough to shoot a questioning look at his brother. "Are we going someplace?"

Elmo made a *tisk*ing sound with his tongue, shook his head, and looked up at the sky. "We can't stay here," he explained patiently. "This is on the trail to town. Sooner or later somebody's gonna miss them two, and they'll come right down this trail looking for them."

His face blank as a new snowdrift, Lester bobbed his head up and down like a woodpecker building a new home. "Yep, that's sure enough right," he agreed. A look of utter concentration on his face, he licked his pinky, then stuck it in his ear, digging like a man looking for water. "Say, Elmo, what are we gonna do with big foot over here?"

Elmo studied me and rubbed his narrow chin. "Now, I been thinking on that, but I ain't come up with anything yet," he admitted. "I reckon we'll just have to tote him along."

Lester finally finished cleaning the wax out of his ears, wiping his hands on his shirt front. "You know, I been studying on that," he announced. "We wouldn't have to kill him. We could just haul him over to that woman. Let her do her own killing. We ketched him. That ought to be worth something."

A woman! My head snapped up so fast, I banged my head against the tree. I scrambled my brain for a woman that might want to do me harm, but my memory fired blanks. To tell the truth, I didn't know many women, and while some of them didn't care for me, I couldn't think of a single one that would go to all this trouble and expense just to hurt me. Most of them were tightwads, like Iris Winkler, for instance.

I started to ask a question, then snapped my mouth closed. I didn't want to let these two know that I had caught on to their little slip of the tongue. Besides, I had a notion that I might learn more by keeping quiet.

Elmo paced around, contemplating Lester's idea. He scraped his boots in the dirt and scratched his armpit. I could tell Elmo favored the idea, but I reckon he woulda liked it a whole bunch more if he had come up with it. "I've done some thinking on that my own-self," Elmo replied with a heavy sigh. "It sounds good, but I still ain't sure that's the way to go. I'll have to do some more thinking.''

"Sure, sure," Lester replied, never taking his eyes off the grub.

Iris let out a snort and branded them with a look that woulda put a chill in a polar bear. "If you two know what's good for you, you'll let me go this instant!"

Lester drew himself up to his full height and looked down his crooked nose at her. He pointed a shaky finger at Iris. "You best just keep your yap shut, or I'll stick that gag back in!"

"You wouldn't dare!" Iris snapped, her eyes blazing pure fire. "I swear, when I get loose, I'm gonna peel your hide off in strips and feed it to the birds!"

Lester swallowed hard and edged around to the other side of the fire. "You watch your mouth or you won't get no vittles." That didn't seem to bother Iris none. She kept cussing both of them all the way through the meal.

We had our breakfast, then moved out, traveling due west. I could tell from the baleful looks they kept shooting at Iris that Elmo and Lester were still smarting from the rawhiding the old woman gave them. I reckon, judging from the way they cowered away from her, that they were a little afraid of ol' Iris. Not that I blamed them for that. Iris Winkler could scare the bloomers off the bogeyman.

We rode west well into the afternoon, then turned south. We were skirting the mountains, riding along the edge of the foothills. After a while we came on a high bluff, with a sheer drop. We rode a few minutes along the crest of the bluff, when Elmo suddenly called a halt. He edged his horse up next to Lester's, and the two of them went to whispering like a couple of old hens at a tea party.

"What fool thing do you think they have in mind this time?" Marie asked, but I could only shrug. Iris didn't even bother with that. She just glared at the two brothers, looking mad enough to bite the tail off a brass monkey.

"Hey!" she yelled in a shrill voice, and I could see Lester and Elmo's shoulders hump like they'd been shot in the back with an arrow. "I'm thirsty. Get me a drink."

"Yes, ma'am," Lester mumbled hurriedly. He jumped off his horse and practically tore the saddle loose from his horse as he jerked the canteen off the saddlehorn. "Here you go, ma'am," he offered, holding the canteen up to her. I guess Iris had put the fear into them boys, judging from the nice way they were treating her now. I coulda told them it wouldn't do them any good. That woman had a memory that woulda put an elephant to shame, and she could hold a grudge with the best of them.

His whole body jerked as she snatched the canteen away from him. She wiped the spout clean with her handkerchief, then took a long, unladylike pull. "Ack!" she sputtered and spat the water full in Lester's face. "This water is warm. I want cold water. Go fetch me some cold water."

Lester rubbed his eyes and swept the water from his

face with his hands. I could see an anger building inside of him, but when he met Iris's frosty gaze, that anger wilted and died. His head hanging, he reached meekly and took the canteen from her. He turned three complete circles, then stopped. He grimaced, pulled on his ear a couple of times, then looked at the ground. "Ah, ma'am, there don't seem to be any fresh water handy."

"That's not my problem!" Iris snapped. "I don't care how you get it, just find me some fresh water."

On his own, I reckon Lester woulda walked plumb to Fort Laramie if that's what it took, but Elmo's shrill voice cut him off. "Hold it!" he screeched. He had his pistol out, the barrel sweeping from horizon to horizon he was shaking so much. His face was the color of a bay horse, but the knuckles that gripped that pistol were dead white. "Lester, you meathead, we kidnapped her. We're in charge here. We don't have to do what she says."

"Oh, yeah, sorry, Elmo, I just forgot," Lester replied. He shoved that canteen back up at Iris. "This is all we got. You can either make do with it or do without." Having spoken his piece, he turned and nodded gravely to Elmo. Boy, was that a big mistake. He sure never shoulda turned his back on Iris 'cause she flung that canteen right back at him. Now, if she was figuring on beaning him in the gourd, her aim was true blue. That canteen bounced off his head with the sound of a mallet hitting a melon.

Lester spun around, grabbing at his gun and growling like an outhouse dog. "Why, you old biddy! I ought to . . . ,'' he grumbled, his threat ending in a bleat as Elmo snatched him by the collar.

"Would you forget about her," Elmo said with a growl, whipped off his hat, and smacked Lester across the shoulders. "We got things to do." Elmo turned to us, still waving that hogleg. "Pile down off them horses," he ordered.

I could only stare. I couldn't believe that even two sharp gents like Elmo and Lester would even consider making camp here. "Hey, Clydesdale. You need a special invite? I said jump down," Elmo threatened, taking a step at me.

I had to shake my head as I swung down. This was no place to camp, there was nothing in the way of shelter, and like Lester noticed, there wasn't even any water. All that was here was a barren wind-swept hill.

I stepped out to the edge of the bluff, intent on seeing if there was a stream of water at the bottom. I was just fixing to lean out and have a look when I heard a yell from behind me. Before I knew what happened, something slammed into me from behind, pushing me toward the edge.

I dug in my heels as Elmo and Lester tried to shove me over. "I hope you can fly, big fellow." Elmo laughed as he strained to shove me over.

My feet were slipping on the slick surface, and I couldn't gain any purchase to shove back. I tried to sit down on them, but Lester was right behind me, shoving on my backside. Lester kept shoving, while Elmo slipped around to the front. He latched onto the front of my shirt and gave a healthy yank. His face turning red, he bowed his back, putting all his weight into pulling me over the edge.

They almost had me when I finally got my feet planted. Once I got my feet under me solid, I hauled back with all my might. I heard Lester squall like a scalded hog as I sat my weight down on him. For good measure, I batted Elmo across the chops. His hands came loose from my shirt and he tipped over backward, flopping like a rag doll. As he disappeared over the edge, I snaked out a hand and snatched a handful of his hair. He let out an ear-splitting howl and grabbed onto my wrist as he dangled over a sheer drop of at least seventy feet. He looked up at me, his eyes bugging out like the chest of that dance-hall girl I'd seen in Denver one time. "Gawd almighty, don't drop me!" he screamed.

Lester danced at my shoulder, plucking at my sleeve. "Mercy sakes, don't drop him!" He turned a couple of circles, waving his arms like he was trying to bring rain. He grabbed my arm again, almost falling to his knees. "Please, mister, pull him up."

"What do you think I'm trying to do," I said and grunted, pushing him away. Now, I reckon if I would just let go, I would have saved the whole country a lot of grief, but I just couldn't do it. Instead, I grabbed his collar with my free hand and tried to flip him up on the bank, but my feet kept slipping. For a wild second, I thought I was going over the edge too. Elmo must have thought so. He went to flapping his arms and legs like he thought flying was his best bet. "Help me, I'm slipping!" I roared at Lester.

Lester grabbed the back of my belt, his feet scrapping on the rock as he pulled back. He didn't have enough lead in his britches to pull me back, but he steadied me enough so I could fling Elmo up on the bank. I didn't get a chance to let him down gently. Mostly I just tossed him like a feed bag. He lit right on his face and skidded a good ten yards. As soon as I let go of Elmo, I went to back-pedaling and believe me, I wasn't stopping for anything. Poor Lester, he couldn't keep up. He lost his feet and went down, and I ran smooth over the top of him.

I tripped and fell, and as I lay on the ground, I thought about grabbing a rock and bashing them two fools' heads in. They were both kinda out of action for a second, and I reckoned I could do the job real easy. I started to do it. My hand closed over the rock, but I couldn't follow through. The thing was, I knew I was liable to kill one or both of them. I could hardly believe it myself. After all the grief and misery they had put me through, I still didn't want to see the two little fellers hurt. Shoot, if I wasn't careful, I would end up liking them. Plumb disgusted by that thought, I growled and flung the rock away, and then my chance to escape was gone.

Lester was getting to his feet, blood oozing from a skinned spot on his neck where my spur raked. He had his gun out and believe me, he wasn't happy. "Why'd you have to go and do that fer?" he asked and dabbed daintily at his neck with his free hand. He started to say something else, then stopped and snapped his pistol up. "Hey! How'd you get untied?"

Huh? I had to look down at my hands before I realized what he said was true: my hands were free. The cord they'd used to tie me lay in frayed pieces around my wrists. "I musta broke them when I snagged onto your brother," I replied with a shrug.

"Broke 'em?" Lester echoed unbelievingly. He looked me up and down. "What the heck have they been feeding you anyway?"

I ignored the question, watching as a shaken Elmo climbed to his feet. He wobbled on rubbery legs, shying back from the edge. "Never mind that. Let's get going," he said, his face ghostly.

Elmo never said another word until we camped for the night. While Lester supervised Marie as she cooked supper, Elmo put me to tending the horses. He held his rifle loosely and leaned against a tree as he watched me work. I stripped off the saddles and slipped the hobbles on the horse. When I finished, I started to head back to the fire, but he jabbed me in the gizzard with that rifle. "Just a minute," he said gruffly.

I stopped, my hands on my hips as I wondered what crazy thing he had in mind now. One thing you had to say about Elmo, he was a persistent son of a gun. He never gave up on a notion.

"Just wanted to say," he started, then looked at the ground. "I reckon you saved my life," he said slowly.

"I didn't think about it; I just done it," I replied uncomfortably.

"Makes no matter," Elmo declared hotly. "You saved my bacon, no two ways about it." He studied the ground, drawing circles in the dust with the toe of his boot. "I don't reckon it would hardly be right for me to kill you now, nor turn you over to that woman."

"What woman?" I asked matter-of-factly.

"The one with the gold . . . ," Elmo started to say, then his mouth snapped shut so fast I could hear his teeth click. "Oh, no, you don't," he sputtered. "You tried to trick me!" he accused, then a smirk replaced the hot expression on his face. "But I was too smart for you. Now don't be asking no more questions about her. It wouldn't be right for me to say anything," he said, shaking a finger in my face.

"If you want to thank me for saving your life, tell me about the woman."

Elmo was already shaking his head. "Nope, can't do that, but what I will do is let you go in the morning."

"How about the two ladies? Are you going to let them go?" I asked.

Elmo shook his head emphatically. "Cain't do that. Since we're letting you go, we gotta find a way to make some money. I figure somebody will pay to get them two back. I don't have the foggiest idea why, but I know that's the way things work."

"Elmo, I'm the sheriff in these parts. I'll have to come chasing after you."

"Sure, sure, you gotta do your job," Elmo agreed solemnly. " 'Course you know that once I let you go, I figure that makes us even-steven." Elmo drew himself up to his full height and gave me a stern look. "If we ketch you again, we won't show no mercy."

Trying to match Elmo's seriousness, I nodded at him. "A man's gotta do what a man's gotta do," I agreed.

Dang right!'' Elmo said, then pointed to the fire with his rifle. "Now, let's go get some grub."

True to his word and despite Lester's protests, Elmo let me go the next morning. 'Course, being Elmo, he couldn't do it the normal way.

"Lester, take the sheriff's horse and lead him a couple of miles away and tie it up," he ordered.

"Aw, come on, Elmo. Why do we have to let him go?" Lester whined.

"Never mind all the sniffling. I done made up my mind and that's that. Now take his horse, while I tie him up."

Lester jerked off his hat and threw it on the ground. Cursing steadily, he kicked the hat several times. "Elmo, I never had ten thousand dollars," he whined.

"Go," Elmo growled, picking up a piece of rope.

"All right, I'm going," Lester said, then stopped. "Say, how come we're doing all this?" he asked, scratching his head.

"So he can't follow us. It'll take him awhile to get loose and get to his horse, and by then we'll be long gone," Elmo answered.

"Say now, that's right good thinking," Lester agreed as he bent over to pick up his hat. "You be sure and tie him good; he can break ropes, you know."

After the pair rode away with Iris and Marie in tow, I went to work on them ropes holding me. It took me till almost noon to finally get free. I scavenged around the camp, but they hadn't left so much as a scrap of food. I cursed that danged Lester, for I knew he was responsible for that. The man ate like a ravenous hog.

Giving up on finding any grub, I slung my saddle over my shoulder and took off, walking toward my horse. I wasn't near halfway when my shoulder started aching from toting that saddle. I shook my head. Them two buffoons couldn't get anything right. If they had any sense, they would put my saddle on my horse so I wouldn't have to carry it.

I walked several more yards before it hit me. I didn't have to carry this saddle. I could dump it and bring the horse back to the saddle. That's what I did, but it was time-consuming. By the time I got my horse saddled and was ready to move out, the biggest share of the afternoon was gone.

I sat on my horse, looking down the trail Elmo, Lester, and the two women took. A sense of duty tugged at me, urging me to go after them. They had a big lead, and the chances of me catching up with them were mighty slim. Besides, I didn't have a gun. Without a weapon, I'd have to pull something mighty fancy to rescue them women. Not that I really feared for their safety. I figured Elmo and Lester were more afraid of them women than the other way around. I imagined that if any harm came to either Marie or Iris it would be some kind of bumbling accident.

So, with a load of guilt riding on my shoulders, I pointed my horse in the direction of Whiskey City and gigged him into a trot. To relieve my guilt, I reminded myself that there was a price on my head and I was unarmed. So far, the only takers on the bounty had been a crotchety, broken-down old man and the two biggest yahoos in the world, but I knew my luck couldn't hold forever. Sooner or later, somebody good was going to come looking for that ten grand. And, of course, there was always Nick Oakley roaming around out there. No, sir, it wouldn't be good for me to be traipsing around the country unarmed. It's been my experience that if you go hunting trouble, you usually find it.

The guilt was still spurring me as the sun sank and darkness began to claim the land. It was the guilt that kept me in the saddle even though I was tired and wanted to stop. Well, I sure shoulda stopped.

I was riding with my head down, my mind on my problems and not paying attention, when I ran right smack dab into it, namely, the twin barrels of a short, wicked shotgun.

Chapter Nine

Behind that shotgun was the weathered, unsmiling face of one Cimarron Bob. His warped hands clutched that shotgun like it was a hot branding iron, but his gnarled, bent finger was jammed in the trigger guard. "Everybody in the country has been looking for you, and I'm the one that finally found you." A smile finally cracked across his face, but it wasn't a nice smile and did very little to cheer me. "I was afraid that Nick Oakley would find you first and stretch your hide."

"And now you're going to do the job?" I asked bitterly, my eyes locked on the muzzle of that gun.

Cimarron Bob chuckled dryly, but his eyes remained cold and steady. "If I had come out here to kill you, you'd be living next door to a gopher right now." He swore and spat in the dirt. "You was wandering around like some kind of dopey-eyed school-girl. I coulda killed you plumb easy.''

I could only sigh and look at the sky. I knew what was coming next. "So now you want *me* to kill *you*,'' I said tiredly.

Cimarron Bob snorted and started to put the shotgun down. The only problem was, old Bob's hands weren't as nimble as they used to be. As he tried to pull his stumpy finger out of the trigger guard, the dang thing hung on the trigger. Well, the short of the whole deal was, that blamed gun went off right in my face. The blast of that shotgun sucked the wax right out of my ears and scalded my face, whipping the hat right off my head.

For a second, my hair stood on end and my eyes snapped wide open as I shrank in the saddle. I swallowed several times, but I still couldn't force down the lump in my throat.

Cimarron Bob finally got rid of that gun; then the old codger busted out laughing. And you know something, for the first time since I known him, shoot, maybe for the first time in his life, Cimarron Bob looked happy. Still laughing, he wiped a tear from his eye and slapped his thigh. "You should see your face. You look like you just bit into a cow pie,'' he roared, then was struck by another fit of laughing. "Aw, don't worry, you ain't hurt none,'' he managed to say between hacks.

Well, by then, I'd pretty much figured that one out by myself. Still, I was poking and prodding around with my fingers just to make sure. I didn't find any blood gushing, so I reckoned I would live. Then I started to get mad. "Why, you grizzled up old sidewinder, you like to killed me!" I exploded.

Slowly the laughter drained off old Bob's face and he looked down at his hands. "I reckon you're right," he said softly, a note of bitterness creeping into his words. Cursing under his breath, he slapped the free end of his reins against his thigh. "I'm old and washed up. I reckon it woulda been best for all if you would have just killed me the other day."

Dang him! Now why did he have to go and say that? Here I was good and mad at him, and with good reason I might add, and now he was making me feel sorry for him. I mean, he was the one that like to blowed my head off, and now here I was feeling bad for getting mad about it.

Cimarron Bob's old chicken neck popped as he shook his head sadly. "You best just shoot me now and save us all a lot of grief."

"I thought you were going to do yourself in. Whatever happened to that notion?" I asked gruffly.

Cimarron Bob hung his head, mumbling as he talked. "Well, that wasn't as easy as I thought. I tried to just lay down and die, but it never happened." All of a sudden, Cimarron Bob's head snapped up and his voice grew stronger. " 'Course, I couldn't concentrate proper. That danged girl of yourn kept pestering me. She even brought me lemonade. Well, we got to talking and like a fool I listened to her."

"What do you mean?" I asked and I couldn't help wishing that Eddy would have just left well enough alone and let the old man die in peace. At least he would be out of my hair.

"She kept harping on the fact that I wasn't finished yet. She kept telling me that I should help you with the trouble you've been having."

As Cimarron Bob's words trailed off, I felt a flash of resentment at Eddy. Why'd she have to go and tell him that for? Now, I'd be saddled with the old coot. But I reckon that was womenfolk for you. I mean, they can't help it, I suppose. They just naturally have to meddle in other folks' affairs. With a start, I snapped out of my daydreamings, as I realized Cimarron Bob was talking again.

"Now I know she meant for me to just give you advice, but then I got to thinking. Well, I reckoned that maybe I could comb Nick Oakley outta your hair for you. I never did care for him anyway. So I came looking for him."

"You needn't have bothered. I can handle Oakley," I replied stiffly.

For a second, I thought old Bob would laugh again, but instead, he snorted and spat on the ground. "That's a hoot. If I'd been Oakley, you'd be explaining your sins to Saint Peter right now," he grumbled. He rubbed his chin, his washed-out blue eyes boring into me. "You know, maybe that girl was right. I reckon I can help you some after all."

"Maybe you can," I admitted, mostly just to shut him up. "But right now, I have to get to town."

"What for?" Bob asked as I swung down to retrieve my hat. Just seeing my hat was enough to put a shake in my joints. The crown of that hat looked like a pack of dogs had been at it. That's how close I came to cashing in my chips. "What's in town?" Bob repeated, a note of irritation riding in his tone.

Picking up my hat, I explained about Lester and Elmo and the kidnapping of Marie and Iris. "I've got to get into town and round up some guns, then go after them," I finished.

"To heck with that!" Cimarron Bob said, his old eyes glowing brightly. "I got a spare pistol and you can use my rifle. I'll stick with this baby," he said and patted the shotgun while I cringed away. "Don't you fret a bit. We'll find them two ladies. I may be old, but I can still foller a trout upstream."

Now, I had serious doubts about that. In his younger days, I reckon old Bob coulda backed that brag up, but now, I'd bet he couldn't spot an elephant track in a snowbank. Shoot, I wasn't even sure he could see the ground, much less spot a track. Although the old goat had a point, the quicker we got on the trail, the better chance we had of catching them. And I could track a mite myself.

"We haven't got any supplies. We might be on the trail several days and we ain't gonna have time to stop and do any hunting. We're liable to get a bit hungry," I said, mostly thinking out loud.

Bob pursed his lips, thinking it over. "You're right about that," he admitted slowly. "Is there a ranch close by?"

"There's Bobby Stamper's place. We could swing

by there, stock up on some grub, then cut across county and pick up the trail.''

I guess he liked the idea because he took off without a word. I hurried to catch up, then adjusted his course to take us in the direction of Bobby and Betsy's place. ''You said something about a pistol and a rifle,'' I reminded after getting him pointed in the right direction. Without a word, he passed them over and we rode into the gathering night.

Despite the darkness that closed in around us, we rode quickly. Still, it was well past midnight when we rode up to Bobby's place. Just the sight of the place brought back a flood of memories. This was my parents' old place, the place where I grew up. I was some surprised at the amount of fixing up Bobby had done. He'd fixed up the old house and even done some work on the barn. Yes, sir, for a man who always appeared as lazy as cold syrup, Bobby had sure done a pile of work.

We unsaddled our horses and turned them into the corral, then trooped up to the house. Old Bob told me that Bobby had taken Betsy into town to be with her father, so we just marched inside the house, not expecting anyone to be home. We barely poked our snouts inside before a bullet clipped the doorjamb above our heads.

As that bullet smacked into the jamb over my head, the first thought that came to mind was to turn tail and run. Now, I saw no reason to argue with that line of thinking, but I couldn't run. That dang Cimarron Bob was right behind me and he wasn't moving. I swear, trying to move him was like rassling a gorilla in a flour barrel. As I tried to shove him back out the door, I heard the sound of a gun being cocked in the dark house behind me.

"Unless you boys want to get yourselves shot, just stand still."

I stopped shoving against old Bob and turned my head. "Bobby, is that you? What are you doing here?" I asked.

"Last time I checked, I lived here," Bobby said, stepping out from behind the big iron cooking stove. He eased the hammer down on his pistol and dropped it into the holster.

"We thought you was in town," I explained as Stamper lit a lamp.

"I might say the same thing about you. When me and Betsy got to town, we figured you and Marie would already be there, but you weren't. So I went looking for you."

"We ran into some trouble," I replied and dropped into a chair. While I told the story, Bobby slapped a pot of leftover stew on the stove to heat.

"Shoot, I never even noticed Iris was gone," Bobby commented as I finished my story. Which wasn't all that surprising, most folks tried to avoid the old bat. "You think they are still safe and sound?" he asked as he dished up three bowls of the stew.

"Sure," I said, taking the bowl he handed to me. "How's old man Wiesmulluer?"

"He's getting more cantankerous by the day, so I reckon he's getting better," Bobby replied and shoved a bowl of stew across the table to Cimarron Bob. "I sure would hate to be them two hillbillies once he gets up and around."

"You got that right," I mumbled, so tired I was about ready to fall asleep on the spot. Without hardly knowing what I was doing, I shoveled a spoonful of that stew into my mouth. Well, that woke me right up. Eating that stew was like eating gunpowder and chasing it down with cheap whiskey. "What the devil is this?" I croaked.

"Never mind, just eat," Bobby growled. "Betsy's still learning to cook. Don't worry, you'll get used to it."

"I don't want to get used to it," I declared pushing the bowl away.

Cimarron Bob leaned down close to his bowl and took a careful taste. His head snapped up so fast it nearly came off his rickety old neck. "I just decided that I want to live and now you expect me to eat this?" he growled.

Bobby looked like he was going to get mad, then shrugged and reached behind him on the counter. He came back with a couple of clothespins, tossing one apiece to me and Cimarron Bob. "Here, put these on your noses. It helps a bunch if you can't smell it."

Well, he was right about that, but even though I was starved, I still couldn't manage to put the whole bowl away. Having ate all we could stand, we turned in, wanting to get an early start the next morning.

It was still dark when we rolled out. While Cimarron Bob stomped around trying to get his old joints loosened up, I saddled some horses and Bobby packed us some grub. As the sun came up, we rode out of the yard. By noon, we'd picked up the trail and were beginning to close the gap.

We were starting to feel pretty good about ourselves, but as evening came on, a bank of black clouds rolled over the mountains from the west.

"We best shake a leg," Cimarron Bob said, lifting his horse into a trot. "If it starts raining now, we can just forget about finding them women."

He was sure enough right about that. Now I don't like doing it, but I got to admit that I was impressed with Cimarron Bob. While he couldn't do much on the ground, he was good as they come on a horse. Moreover, he had an uncanny feel for where the trail would go. Anytime the tracks grew dim, he knew right where to go to pick the trail up again.

Yes, sir, Cimarron Bob had saved us a lot of time, but even he couldn't hold back the rain. It started slowly, just a few drops, but then the skies opened up and it poured.

We took shelter under a small overhang, squatting on our heels as we watched it pour. Nobody said a word, but we were all thinking the same thing, we might as well head back to town. We had failed.

Chapter Ten

Whiskey City was buzzing with activity when we straggled into town. A crowd of folks was gathered in a tight bunch in front of the saloon. Mr. Andrews stood on the boardwalk making a speech like some kind of soapbox politician. As he spotted us, his words trailed off and he stared open-mouthed down the street at us. Well, I suppose we were a sight to behold. We'd been rained on, caught in a dust storm, and slept in our wet clothes. All in all, we looked a mite rough.

"Where the devil have you boys been?" Andrews demanded.

"Never mind that," Eddy snapped, shoving folks aside so she could get to the front of the crowd. "Where's Mother?"

I couldn't bring myself to answer, nor could I meet

her fiery gaze. I stared down at the scuffed toes of my boots, wishing I could sink right in the ground.

"She and Teddy were kidnapped," Cimarron Bob said, his tone daring someone to make something of it.

"How did you happen to get away, and what happened to mother?" Betsy demanded, her jaw set firm as she stepped up beside her sister.

I couldn't meet their eyes. Right then, I wished we had never come back to town at all. For a wild second, I thought about jumping on my horse and taking out. "I got away," I stammered. "They sorta let me go."

"What do you mean you got loose? Why would they let you go?" Eddy demanded as she and Betsy both took a step at me.

"Well, I reckon you might say that I saved one of the kidnapper's lives, so they let me go," I answered, then cringed away from the outburst I knew was coming.

It didn't come right away. I guess Eddy and Betsy were too surprised to say anything right away. They—shoot, the whole crowd—stared at me in shock. Mr. Claude recovered first. "Who were these kidnappers?"

"They were the same two fellers that shot Mr. Wiesmulluer," I replied, my tone small as a mouse squeak.

Looking like a man who'd just taken a punch, Burdett shook his bull head. "Well, why in the name of Harriet's hash didn't you just let the slimy polecat cash in his chips?"

"You mean to stand there and say that you saved the life of the man that shot my father and kidnapped my mother?" Betsy asked like she couldn't believe her ears.

"I don't know," I mumbled miserably. "He fell over a cliff and I snatched him and yanked him back. I didn't think about it. I just did it."

"How did he come to fall off a cliff?" Mr. Andrews wanted to know.

"He was trying to push me over and slipped." Again I got them blank stares of disbelief. "You had to be there," I explained lamely.

"Never mind about him," Gid Stevens howled. "What about my Iris? She's been missing for days."

"Yeah, and it's been downright pleasant for days too," said Joe Havens, who owned the saloon.

That sure put ol' Gid's kettle on the boil. He dove into the crowd, his fists swinging as he tried to reach Joe. "Hold it, Gid!" I yelled, snagging him by the collar and hauling him back. "There's no need to get all riled up. Iris is fine. The kidnappers have her."

"What!" Gid screamed and turned to face me. "How can you say she's all right if she's been kidnapped?"

Aw, heck, they's harmless," I assured him, waving off his concerns.

"They already shot Daddy," Eddy reminded. "It seems to me they are dangerous enough."

It was shaping up to be a first-class argument, when we heard a yell from the edge of town. As one, we whirled to look down the street just past Burdett's livery stable. Riding in a tight group came Lester and Elmo, with Marie and Iris out front. ''Now, don't no-body go gettin' nervous. We're plumb friendly,'' Elmo called.

Nobody paid much mind to his words. A dozen guns were directed at the two brothers, my own pistol among them. ''What do you two want?'' I growled.

Elmo sat straight in the saddle and puffed out his chest. ''We came to escort these two fine ladies back to where they belong,'' he said and looked mighty proud of himself.

''That's right,'' Lester agreed, bobbing his head up and down like a pump handle.

Still setting in the saddle like a strutting peacock, Elmo rubbed his chin. ''Now, I know everybody likely wants to buy us a drink for seeing these fine ladies home safely, but we ain't got the time right now. 'Course, if you was inclined to pay us for our trouble we'd take some cash.''

Iris snorted rather indelicately and started to say something, but Lester reached out and slapped her horse on the rump. Her words was cut off in mid-tirade as she latched onto the saddle horn and fought the bucking animal. Lester grabbed her bridle, but he wasn't doing a lot to calm the horse. ''Whoa, ma'am, you best be careful,'' he said.

''Well, like we said, we got things to do, so we'll be moseying along,'' Elmo said hurriedly and started to wheel his horse around.

''Hold it, Elmo!'' I cried out, stepping away from the crowd as Elmo's shoulders hunched up. ''We have a couple of things to discuss,'' I added and headed my pistol in his direction.

''Such as what?'' Elmo demanded surlily.

''Such as the shooting of Karl Wiesmulluer,'' I countered gently.

Elmo cursed bitterly and threw his hat on the ground. ''Now, dang nab it, we done tol' you that was an accident!''

''That's right,'' Lester allowed defiantly. ''How many times do we have to tell you, we didn't mean to plug that old geezer. We was aiming at you.''

''That ain't exactly legal either. Shooting at a sheriff, I mean,'' I informed them.

''Legal shmeagal,'' Elmo grunted. ''There's a price on your head. We was just trying to earn an honest living. Ain't no crime in that.''

I swear, these boys best stay away from the swimming hole, 'cause they sure enough had rocks in their heads. ''Any time you shoot somebody around here, we call it a crime,'' I said, rubbing the spot between my eyes, which was starting to ache all of a sudden.

''Yeah? Well, what about him?'' Lester asked, pointing a shaky finger at Cimarron Bob. ''That old goat has killed more folks than smallpox.''

''That ain't any of your concern. We ain't talking about him, we're talking about you,'' I barked and motioned toward the jail with my pistol. ''Now get going.''

Lester squinted his eyes and crossed his arms across his chest. ''Ain't gonna do it and you can't make me,'' he allowed, poking out his bottom lip.

I sighed. Couldn't anything ever be simple with these two? "Mr. Stamper, would you mind giving me a hand with these two?" I asked.

Bobby smiled and passed his reins to Cimarron Bob. "I'd be happy to."

Lester and Elmo edged their horse away, their shifty eyes scuttling from me and Bobby to the dozen or so guns trained on them. "I'm warning you, we can play rough if we have to," Elmo threatened.

His blustering didn't bother Bobby Stamper, not in the least. Now, Bobby didn't bother with any fanfare. He just grabbed Elmo's stirrup and heaved. Bleating loudly, Elmo toppled from the saddle, landing smack-dab on his bean.

While Lester stared stupidly at his brother, I grabbed the front of his shirt and drug him from the saddle. He kicked and screamed the whole time I drug him over to the jail, and Bobby did the same with Elmo.

We tossed them in the cell, then I dug a bottle out of my desk. "I don't know about you, but I could sure use a bracer," I said, holding up the bottle. The smile that split across Bobby's face was all the answer I needed. I fished a couple of glasses out of the desk drawer and blew the dust out of them. I pulled the cork outta the bottle with my teeth, then splashed a healthy slug into the bottom of each glass.

"Say, Sheriff, we could sure use a snort of that there trantular juice," Elmo suggested, rubbing his hands together greedily.

"I could use a little peace and quiet. So why don't you just sit down and be quiet?"

"Now, Teddy, that ain't hardly neighborly," Bobby said, a sly smile playing on his lips. "Ain't no harm in seeing that them boys are good and comfortable."

I didn't rightly know what Bobby had in mind, but I could see that something was brewing in his head. With a shrug, I refilled our glasses, then carried the bottle back to the cell and held it out. I swear, Elmo like to taken a couple of my fingers when he snatched that bottle away from me.

Immediately, the two brothers began arguing over the bottle. Ignoring the ruckus, I dropped back into my chair and looked questioningly across the desk at Bobby. He grinned at me, then took a drink. "You know, a little of this might loosen their tongues. We might even finagle the name of that woman who put the reward on your head."

A smile grew on my lips. "That ain't bad thinking," I acknowledged and took a peak over my shoulder at the cell. Lester and Elmo were taking to that bottle like pigs to a slop trough. Between the two of them, they'd pretty much polished the thing off. "Looks like it might be working," I commented.

I poked around in the bottom of my desk and found another bottle. It was old as the hills. It'd been in the desk when I took over the sheriffing duties. I picked up the bottle and wiped the dust from it, then held it up to the light. More than likely the stuff had curdled, but I didn't figure them boys would be all that choosy. I laid it on the floor and gave it a small shove toward the cell. Like bird dogs on the point, their heads snapped up as they watched the bottle roll slowly toward them. As it stopped against the barred cell door, they both made a dive for it.

After several more drinks, Elmo and Lester were singing and looked to be happy as jaybirds. Bobby eased back to the cell and leaned casually against the bars. "Say, boys, it 'pears your bottle is about empty."

Lester glanced down at the near-empty bottle in his hand, his face turning sad as a coon dog's with a sore paw. "Now, that's a downright shame," he mumbled.

"We could mosey over to the saloon and bring you back another bottle," I suggested.

Lester took a quick drink and nodded eagerly as Elmo stepped up to the bars, his tongue hanging out. "Shoot, we could even take you over there," Bobby said.

"Yeah, yeah. Let's go," Elmo cried, shaking the bars hard enough to bring dust trailing down from the rafters.

"Sure, sure, we can go, but first, we need you to answer a couple of questions," I said, watching their reactions.

A wary hunted look crossed their faces as they backed up a step. "What kind of questions?" Elmo asked, his words already starting to slur together.

"Don't tell 'em nothin', Elmo. You cain't trust no lawman," Lester bawled.

"Look, fellas, all I need is the name of the woman that put the price on my head," I coaxed.

"We ain't telling," Elmo grunted.

"All you have to do is tell us the name and we'll take you over to the saloon and set you up with a round of drinks," Bobby told them. He leaned up against the bars, winking broadly at the two brothers.

"You might even be able to escape," I suggested. "In a crowded place like the saloon, a couple of slick fellers like yourselves would be awful hard to keep up with."

That pleased them, I could see, but they didn't see fit to cough up the name, so I switched tactics. "How come you decided to let Iris and Mrs. Wiesmulluer loose? I thought you were going to ransom them?"

Elmo shook his head mournfully. "That were a bad idea. Them women were no end of trouble."

"Bring me water. Wash that plate. This blanket is filthy," Lester squeaked in a false high tone. "Wasn't nothing we did ever good enough for them." He cut his eyes up at the ceiling, then slapped the side of his face and took a quick drink. "Women!" he exclaimed disgustedly. "We was glad to get rid of them!"

"We got to thinking, who in their right mind would pay to get that old battle-ax back," Elmo said in agreement.

"Yeah, the only way we could make money is if somebody paid us to keep her, and there ain't that much money in the world," Lester declared, a shudder ripping through his body."

"And that other one. I didn't care for the way she kept looking at me. She was up to something, I could tell," Elmo explained.

"The woman who offered the money to kill me, what was she like?" I asked casually.

"She was . . . ," Lester started, but never got a chance to finish, as Iris stormed through the door, towing Gid behind her. She looked to be in a good mood . . . well, good for her anyway. That good mood did a bellyflop when she saw us sharing a drink with Elmo and Lester.

"I should have known!" she snapped and stomped her foot. "The minute I turn my back, you're in here drinking and consorting with the enemy."

Both Elmo and Lester scuttled to the farthest corner of the cell. Elmo pointed a shaky finger at her. "Sheriff, you get her outta here," he said, his voice quivering a mite.

"Iris, do you mind? We're trying to talk business here," I said patiently.

"No, we ain't," Elmo declared, watching Iris the way a rabbit watches a coyote.

Elmo looked ready to stand his ground, but poor Lester folded his tent. "All right, Sheriff. We'll tell you what you want to know, just keep her away from us," he sputtered, all wide-eyed.

"You'll tell me about the woman?" I asked suspiciously.

"Sure, you just tell her go get," Lester squawked.

"Whoa, wait a minute," Elmo said, and held up his hand. "You're still going to let us go like you promised?"

Old Iris's mouth dropped open wide enough to shove a watermelon pie in sideways. Her eyes blazed fire and her jaw sawed back and forth but no sound came out. I glanced at Elmo, wishing he was closer so I could splatter him a good one. For all I knew, this was just the calm before the storm; Iris was about to blow her stack any second.

She didn't disappoint me either. That old woman lit into me and Bobby like we was a couple of cur dogs. And let me tell you, the words she used weren't nothing you would hear at a young ladies' finishing school either.

After giving us a right good cussin', even Iris had to stop and suck some air. But once she got her lungs primed, she was ready to make another stab at it. "Theodore Cooper, has that pea brain of yours rolled out of your ear?" she roared, clenching her fists at her side. "These two blackguards cruelly abducted me out of my flower bed and subjected me to unspeakable horrors, and now you want to let them go?"

Now, if the truth be told, I reckon it went the other way. I 'magine she tormented Elmo and Lester, but I had the good sense to keep such notions to myself. "I know, ma'am. And believe me, I'm truly sorry about what happened to you," I said gently.

"You should be!" she snapped. "If you would have been here in town doing your job, instead of out gallivanting around the country, this might not have happened."

"Did you come here for something special?" I asked, hoping to get rid of her.

"You dang right I did!" she sputtered. "Somebody's stealing from our store!"

Our store? The way she talked, you'd think she and Gid was already hitched. "I'll look into it first chance I get," I promised.

"You'll look into it right now, buster!" she snapped.

"I'm just a little busy questioning these prisoners at the moment," I told her, trying to be reasonable.

"What's to ask them? They kidnapped me, you know that. Just throw them in the pokey and forget about them," Iris said with a shrug.

"They know who put the reward on my head. I'd like to find out who wants me dead and put a stop to it before someone shoots me."

"Wouldn't be no great loss if you ask me. You ain't no great shakes as a sheriff," Iris said with a sniff.

"That don't matter. I said I'd look into your problem and I will, when I get good and ready," I snapped without thinking.

She pursed her lips and color shot into her face. For a second, I thought I'd pushed her over the edge and she would blow up on me again. But for once, Gid showed some backbone. He didn't come up with his courage all at once, it took some hemming and hawing. He jammed his hands down in his pockets, then pulled them out again and shifted his feet. "Now see here, Teddy. I know a few paltry items stolen from our store doesn't sound like much to you, but it means a lot to us."

That was the problem with being sheriff in a place like Whiskey City: always one headache after another. "All right," I said heavily. "I'll look into it and see what I can find out," I promised, trying to shoo them out the door.

Iris was gonna have none of that. She crossed her arms and planted her feet. Shooing her away was like driving hogs. "Oh, no you don't," she screeched, getting jaw-to-jaw with me, which was quite a feat considering the difference in our heights. "You're not going to sweep this under the rug, just so you can get back to your drinking!"

I sighed and looked to Bobby for some support. He weren't no help at all. He just leaned against the bars, looking like he swallowed a live chicken. Fine way to treat a friend, laughing when he should be lending a hand.

"I got a good idea who's been doing the stealing, and I want you to go arrest him," Iris declared.

"Who might that be?" I asked, mildly interested.

"That filthy Cimarron Bob, that's who!" Iris bellowed and stomped her foot.

"What makes you think that?" Bobby asked, a snicker sneaking out with his words.

Iris branded him with a look that woulda put a preacher man to hunting a bottle. "Well, we didn't start missing things until he showed up, and we all know what kind of a man he is."

"No, pray tell us what kind of man he is," Bobby exclaimed, clapping his hands to his face.

I shot a quick warning to him with my eyes. Now, Bobby Stamper might have once been a bank robber, and he might have made fools of the lawmen and the

Army all up and down the frontier, but even he was no match for Iris Winkler.

She jabbed a bony finger in his face, then grabbed his ear and yanked him down to her level. "You best watch yourself, buster!" she hissed, then turned her wrath at me. "And you, sonny, you best do something about that Cimarron Bob, or I'll do something about you."

I started to breathe again as she turned to leave, but just as I was starting to relax, the old bat whirled back to face me. "And if you let these two heathens go, I'll have your hide!" She jabbed a bony finger at poor Elmo and Lester like it was a lightning rod. "And if you two have any thoughts of escaping, you best know that I'll hunt you down like the dogs you are. I got myself a buffalo gun, and I ain't afraid to use it."

The silence after the door closed behind her was so quiet you could hear the grass growing outside of town. I looked at the door, clenching my fists and growling under my breath. Bobby laughed and clapped me on the back. "Easy, big fella," he said.

"Shut up! You didn't help matters any," I growled and smacked my fist into my palm.

Bobby laughed again, squeezing my shoulder. "Aw, don't worry about it. If it came down to a fight, I reckon you could take her."

"I don't know about that," Elmo declared, his eyes wide as a kid's at the circus.

"Never mind about that," I said, pushing Iris out of my mind and jumping to the bars. "I want to know about the woman that put the reward out on me. Who is she?''

Elmo paced back and forth, rubbing his chin. ''Her name was Lilly something or other. Way we heard it, whoever kills you sends word to her in Denver and collects the ten grand,'' he finally said with a shrug.

''Lilly!'' I exclaimed, shooting a glance at Bobby, then swinging back to the two brothers. Lilly Simmons! Turley's so-called wife? I'd bet on it. ''This Lilly, was she a blonde lady, pretty as a paint pony?''

Lester snorted disgustedly. ''How in tarnation should we know. We never saw her, we just heard about the deal on the trail.''

I paced the tiny office, a plan beginning to form in my head. ''I want you guys to do me a favor,'' I said slowly as I made up my mind.

Lester didn't even contemplate it, he just shook his head, while Elmo eyed me with a crafty look on his horse face. ''What would it be worth to you?''

''You want to get out of this jail? Well, if you don't help me, you're gonna be here until you're old as dirt.''

''Now just hold on one gol-durn minute,'' Lester said, plucking at Elmo's sleeve. ''I ain't so all fired sure I want out. Did you hear what that crusty old bat said? She's got herself a buffler gun!''

''We'd be long gone 'fore she even knew. Besides, I doubt if she can shoot that gun,'' Elmo replied as he slapped his brother's hands away. ''Now, Sheriff, what did you have in mind?''

''Elmo, please,'' Lester whined. ''Did you ever see

a man shot with one of them big guns? They'd have to break out a mess of bloodhounds just to sniff out enough of us to bury.''

Elmo snorted and waved off Lester, who paced the cell, mumbling under his breath and kicking the stone floor. ''There ain't no harm in hearing the man out,'' Elmo allowed, licking his lips as a greedy smile spread across his face.

''I want you to send word to Lilly that you killed me and you want her to come here and pay the reward,'' I replied.

Elmo was already shaking his head. ''Now, why would you want us to do that? Even if she falls for it and coughs up the money, she's bound to find out sooner or later that you ain't dead. She'll just send that big ugly son of a gun Nick Oakley after you. She might even sic the polecat on us.''

''No she won't,'' I said, and I couldn't quite keep the pride out of my voice. ''She won't just fork over the money. She'll want to make sure I'm dead first.''

Elmo scratched his chin and spat on the floor. ''Yeah, I reckon you're right about that, but she ain't gonna be happy when she finds out you ain't croaked. We won't get our money.''

''I don't think she has any money to pay you with,'' Bobby told them.

Blank looks on their faces, the two brothers looked at me, their eyes pleading for me to say Bobby had lied. I shook my head sadly. ''I'm sorry, boys, but she rode out of here a few months ago dead broke and with her tail between her legs. I don't see how she could have raised that much money."

Lester hauled off and smacked his brother across the shoulders. "I knew it!" he bellered. "I tol' you we should have never left Denver. We was doing real good picking off travelers."

"Bah, that was peanuts," Elmo said, unfazed. "We couldn't make ten thousand dollars there in ten years."

Lester sneered and clapped his hands in front of Elmo's face. "Would you wake up and smell the breeze coming off the manure pile? We ain't made ten bucks here, and we ain't gonna make ten thousand, neither. We already in jail, and we'll be lucky if that old woman don't skin us alive."

"Shut up, Lester. I'm dickering with the sheriff," Elmo said, shoving his brother away. A sly look on his face, he rubbed his jaw and looked smugly at me. "Now, let's suppose we done what you want and sent that telegram. How much would it be worth to you?"

"I'm letting you out of jail!" I roared, fighting my temper. "Isn't that enough? Don't you know what Iris is going to do when she finds out?"

"She ain't gonna be happy, that's for sure," Bobby agreed solemnly.

Calm as you please, Elmo turned his head up at the ceiling and dug a finger in his ear. "Well now, that ain't my problem." He sat down on the bunk and rested his chin in his hands. "I ain't the one that's got every hard case this side of Hades looking for me. And don't be forgetting about Nick Oakley; he'll be riding into this town soon."

"You're the ones going to jail for a long time," I told them.

Elmo shrugged. "Maybe so, but we'll still be alive and you'll be keeping company with the worms."

"Look guys, I'd like to pay you something, but I don't have any money."

"Hah! That ain't what we heard," Lester declared. "Way we heard it, you aced this lady out of a gold mine and that's why she wants you scotched."

Elmo smiled and placed his hands behind his head as he leaned back. "The way we see it, you got yourself this gold mine and you're rolling in it and we want some of it."

I laughed bitterly; I was rolling in it all right, but it wasn't nearly as pretty as gold and it didn't smell good, neither. That fool gold mine of Turley's was going to be the death of me yet.

Bobby laughed, slapping his leg. "There isn't any gold in that mine. If there was, the man that had it first never woulda let it go."

"What do you think we are, stupid?" Elmo scoffed. "If that mine ain't worth nothing, why would that lady pay all that money to have you killed?"

"I guess she thinks it's still worth something," I said slowly.

Bobby laughed again. "She broke jail and skipped town before we found out the mine was worthless."

"Broke jail!" Lester shouted, jumping a foot into the air. For a second, he waved his hands wildly, then got control of himself. Pasting a casual look on his face, he sauntered to the bars and leaned against them.

He picked dirt from his fingernails, then looked at me out of the corner of his eyes. "How did she manage to break out of this fine jail?"

"She had help. Somebody slipped her the key," I snapped as Lester wilted. "Forget about the mine. It ain't important. In fact, I done sold it. What's important is to get this woman to Whiskey City so I can put a stop to all this."

"What are you gonna do? Shoot her?" Lester asked.

"Of course not!" I snapped and kicked the barred door. I took a deep breath and got control of myself. "I don't rightly know what I'm gonna do. I'll figure it out once she gets here."

"Teddy, I see a little problem with this scheme of yours," Bobby said, leaning against the bars and rolling a smoke. "If you are going to convince Lilly that these two boobs actually killed you, you're gonna have to stay out of sight for a few days."

"Boobs!" Elmo roared, leaping off the bunk. "Who you calling a boob?"

"Shut up, Elmo," I snapped, turning my attention to Bobby. "Stay out of sight? What for? I've got a lot of things to do. Iris and Gid expect me to nab the guy who's been pilfering out of their store; Mr. Burdett needs help and I need to start building me and Eddy's new house."

"Maybe so, but if you want this to work, you're gonna have to lay low," Bobby said with a shrug. "You met Lilly and you know what kind of a woman she is. She's one smart lady, and she ain't about to come riding in here blind. She'll do some checking around first and when she hears that you're still walking around . . .''

He had a point. That Lilly Simmons was a hard woman and sharp as a tack. A man would have to get up awfully early in the morning to pull the wool over her eyes, which was what I was going to try and do. ''OK,'' I agreed with a heavy sigh. ''It'll take a week for her to get here. Where am I going to hide for a week?''

''How about where you're going to build your new house. That's an out-of-the-way spot. You could spend a few days working on your new house. You might want to take these two jokers along to help you.''

I grimaced. I didn't want to baby-sit Elmo and Lester for five minutes, much less a week or more, but Bobby was right. If we didn't keep them under wraps, they'd find a way to louse things up. ''All right, you go with Lester to Central City and send the wire. I'll keep Elmo here and get things ready. When you get back, the three of us will disappear.''

''You might want to take that crusty old gent, Cimarron Bob, with you. He's unpredictable as the wind. If he said anything, it might tip Lilly off. Who knows, he might even throw in with her.''

Well, we made our plans and patted ourselves on the back, telling each other how smart we were. We even had ourselves a drink to toast our brilliant plan. The only thing we didn't know was two men were riding like the devil for Whiskey City. And both of them were going to blow our plans sky high.

Chapter Eleven

I woke up real slow the next morning, a glaring sun beating through my window. My head felt like it was growing, almost to the point it would explode. I tried to swallow, but my tongue felt as thick as a mattress, and my whole mouth tasted like a pack of wild dogs had been sleeping in it. I tell you, this business of questioning prisoners took a lot out of a man.

I stood up and took a few wobbly steps, finding that gravity was a whole bunch stronger than I ever remembered. Staggering to the dresser, I wrapped both arms around the pitcher of water. I started to pick up the glass, then said the heck with that and guzzled straight from the pitcher. That pitcher didn't come close to slaking my thirst, so I pointed the toes of my boots for the café, wanting a bathtub full of coffee.

I didn't make it to the café. I barely made it out of

the room before Bobby cornered me. "You looked a mite peaked this morning," he chirped brightly.

I nearly throttled him. And he woulda deserved it too. Anybody who could bounce outta bed grinning after the night we'd put in didn't deserve to live. I brought my hands up to choke him down, but then said the heck with it. He sure needed it, but I was too pooped to bother. "What do you want?" I asked irritably.

"I busted our two friends out of jail. They're waiting just outside of town for me. You can round up Cimarron Bob and slip out of town, and I'll spread the word you went chasing after them other two."

"You left Elmo and Lester out there by themselves? They likely took off already," I complained.

Bobby smiled and grinned. "I don't think so," he said and from the way he said it, I believed him.

We walked together down the hall to Cimarron Bob's room. I didn't know what I was going to say to him, but I figured that old man would see through a made-up story like it was a picture window. He listened while I told him what we had in mind, his face giving away nothing about his thoughts.

When I finished, he rubbed his jaw, looking up at me with those watery blue eyes. "All right, I'll do it," he said finally. "Mind you, I ain't going along with this because I think this harebrained scheme has any chance of working, but if you're going to build a house, you'll need my help." He stared at my face and rubbed his jaw again. "That girl of yours will be wanting a nice place to live. I reckon I'd best be there to make sure you do things right.''

I looked at Bobby, who grinned back at me. That had gone easier than I ever dreamed. And Cimarron Bob was right, while I'd done some building in my time, I could sure use an experienced hand to coach me along.

A few minutes later me and old Bob rode out of town. I sat a stiff pace, and we rode in silence. Cimarron Bob didn't seem to be in any mood to talk, and the way I felt this morning, that suited me just fine.

When we reached the spot where I planned to build he changed. An excitement seemed to catch him as we went to work. First, we built a makeshift corral and lean-to for the horses. For a gunfighter, Bob was quite a builder. By the end of the first day we pretty much had the corral and the lean-to built. That lean-to wasn't much, just a low, three-sided building, but it would give my stock some shelter until I could build a good barn next summer.

The next morning we started on the house. We had a good start on the job when Bobby rode in with Lester and Elmo two days later. He stayed for a day and helped, and the house began to take shape. We were building a small two-room cabin, leaving so it would be handy to add more rooms later.

That next morning, Bobby left for town and I started on the roof. I was up top, working, when I saw the horse.

The horse came slowly, the rider hunched over the

saddle. His face was buried in the animal's mane, but from the man's build, I guessed it was Bobby Stamper's friend Luther.

I rushed out, stumbling a little as I snatched up the reins. The horse shied a little, but I held tight to the reins with one hand and steadied Luther with the other. As the horse shied, Luther raised his massive, bald head. A slow smile spread across his cracked and bleeding lips. "Teddy," he croaked hoarsely. "I'm glad I found you. I got news for you."

"Never mind that now. Let's get you down," I told him. I couldn't tell how bad the big outlaw was hurt, but his saddle was sticky with drying blood. "You can tell me about it later," I said gently.

"No," Luther said, grabbing my arm. "I know who put the bounty on your head!"

"A woman named Lilly. I know all about it. Now let's get you down and tended to," I said, helping him slide down off the horse. "Lester! Elmo! Haul your scrawny backsides out here!" I bellowed.

Like two prairie dogs, they poked their heads out of the partly finished house. "Whatcha want, Boss?" Lester called.

"Help me get this man inside," I snapped.

Together, we carried Luther inside and eased him into Lester's bed, which was the closest. "Hey, that's my bed!" Lester protested. "How come we got to stick him in bed?"

"What's the difference?" I asked, pulling back Luther's shirt to get a look at his wounds.

"He looks like he might croak any minute. It's gotta

be bad luck to have a body snuff out in your bed," Lester whined.

"Bad luck for him is all. Now, quit your belly-aching and go fetch Cimarron Bob," I barked. I shoved him toward the door, ignoring his yelp as he plowed into the wall.

"I'm a-goin', no need to get all het up," Lester grumbled, rubbing the lump that was rising up on his jaw.

"Go!" I roared, then stabbed a finger at Elmo. "You, get a fire started and heat some water."

While Elmo put a fire together, I ripped loose a piece of Luther's shirt and began swabbing the blood from his chest. As I worked, Luther's brown eyes fluttered open. For a second, they stared blankly up at me, but slowly they came into focus. As he recognized me, he clutched my arm and struggled to sit up. "Teddy, that woman, she's out to get you! She wants you dead!"

"I know. She thinks I stole a gold mine from her."

"No," Luther whispered. He started to say more, but a fit of coughing racked his body and he collapsed back into the bed. "Silver!" he said, reaching both hands up at my face. "Teddy, silver!" With that, his eyes rolled back and he collapsed. His breath seemed to catch in his throat, then stopped altogether.

"Luther!" I shouted and shook his shoulders. The wind eased out of him, then slowly started, sounding hoarse and ragged. I blew out a sigh myself, my shoulders sagging with relief.

"Hey, you dang mullet head!" Cimarron Bob

shouted, his old bones popping as he staggered through the door. "That ain't no way to treat a wounded man. Did you think shaking the fire outta him would help?"

"He just stopped breathing, I didn't know what else to do," I stuttered, wringing my hands. "He's breathing now," I added in my own defense.

"He is?" Cimarron Bob rubbed his chin and looked down at me like he couldn't believe it. Finally, he smiled grimly and shrugged his shoulders. "Well, shoot, I reckon you just happened on a new cure. Now, get back out of the way so I can work."

I gratefully stepped back, watching closely while he worked. It occurred to me that the way folks in these parts kept wandering in front of bullets, I ought to learn something about doctoring. "Is he going to die?" I asked, leaning forward to peer over the old man's shoulder.

"Sure, he is," Cimarron Bob grunted. "Everybody kicks the bucket sometime or another."

"I meant, is he gonna die right now?" I muttered, and balled my hands into fists.

"The only one who's gonna die right now is you, if you don't get your flabby carcass out of my light!"

"Sorry," I mumbled, shuffling my feet as I stepped back. "Is there anything I can do to help?"

For a minute he ignored me, grunting as he worked. "You might make some broth," he replied absently. "Dump in a bucket of salt."

I'd already hustled off to do his bidding; now I stopped and glanced back at him curiously. "Salt?"

"Sure, I heard it was good for blood loss," Cimarron Bob replied with a slight shrug. "I don't rightly know if it works or not, but it can't hurt any. Salt never killed anyone."

Sounded good to me. While old Bob dug out the one bullet that was still inside Luther, I made a broth out of jerky and a couple of hunks of bacon. By the time the broth was ready, Cimarron Bob had the bullet out and the holes plugged, and was using strips cut from a blanket to bandage Luther's chest.

We tried to feed Luther some broth, but the big outlaw wouldn't eat. He just lay there with his eyes closed, muttering. He kept mumbling about some jasper named Thomas and something about the color silver. Every once in a while, he'd scream out my name and warn me to watch out.

Lester looked at me, his long face grave as a tombstone. "You best mind your p's and q's, big man. I reckon Luther here is in the spirit world and seeing the future."

"Huh?" I said and grunted as old Bob snorted and looked away. "Spirit world my backside. I think you plumb went and lost your mind."

Lester squared his shoulders and shot me a haughty look. "It's true. A feller hurt that bad is in touch with the spirits and can see the future. He's trying to tell you something real bad is about to happen to you." Lester stood up and moved several feet away from me, then sat back down. "No offense, but I don't want to be too close to you when it happens," he explained.

"Stop talking nonsense," I said scoffingly, but I couldn't quite ignore the shiver tickling my backbone.

"It ain't nonsense," Lester sputtered defiantly. "Just ask C.B. there. I bet he knows about such things."

"Who's this guy Thomas he keeps harping about?" Cimarron Bob asked, ignoring Lester.

I shrugged and chewed on a piece of jerky. I looked out the hole in the wall that would be the door and watched the sun slowly set. "I don't know who this Thomas might be, but then, I don't know Luther all that well."

"Who gives a hoot about some galoot named Thomas?" Elmo said, his eyes bright. "What I want to know about is that silver he keeps yabbering about. What you reckon that's all about? A cache of silver Spanish coins, maybe?"

"I doubt it," I replied and took another bite of my jerky.

"Ha, you're just trying to throw us off the trail so you can have all them Spanish coins to yourself," Lester accused.

Old Cimarron Bob snorted and shot a disgusted look at the two brothers. "You know, I musta heard a thousand stories about Spanish treasure over the years. Never did hear one single solitary story about anybody ever finding any of it."

"Yeah? Well who asked you, you old goat?" Elmo blustered.

As they jawed back and forth, I closed my eyes. I had to shake my head. That Cimarron Bob was a contrary joker, he actually seemed to enjoy fussin' with them two. Not me—just talking to them set my head to aching something fierce. Pushing the sound of their voices out of my mind, I slowly drifted off to dreamland.

When I woke, I looked out the open door. It was pitch-dark, clouds having rolled in during the night. I couldn't tell what time it was, but it felt very late.

"Water." Hearing the hoarse cry, I sat up and peered through the dark to where Luther lay. "Water," he repeated.

Feeling around with my hands, I found my canteen, then scooted over to the big outlaw. "Here," I said, holding the canteen while he took a long gurgling drink. "You want something to eat?" I asked after he finished.

"No, thanks," Luther said, his voice so weak I could barely hear him. "You know a man named Turley?"

"Yeah, I know him. Why do you ask?"

"You got to find him and warn him. That woman is out to get him too."

"She wants that mine," I said, starting to see things a little more clearly. I looked out at the clouds, thinking it over. "Turley owned the mine before me. I bet she thinks if she gets rid of both of us there wouldn't be anyone to dispute her claim to the mine."

I looked down to see if Luther agreed with me, but the big outlaw had drifted off to sleep again. For a long time, I sat beside him, drumming my fingers on the canteen and staring into the darkness.

Now, I never did figure out if Turley and Lilly were really married or not. She claimed they were and he said they weren't. Neither one of them was famous for telling the truth, so it was heads or tails on which one was telling the truth this time. Not that it really mattered. If she came to town, I reckon Turley would go see her.

All of a sudden, I made a decision. I nestled the canteen next to Luther, so he could find it if he woke back up, then I went outside. Buttoning my coat against the chill in the night air, I hustled out to our makeshift barn and threw a saddle on my horse.

My ol' horse didn't act all that pleased to see me, but I paid that no mind, as I pointed him toward town. A light snow began to fall as we rode. I jerked down my hat and turned up my collar, hunching my shoulders against the cold. I wondered if I was doing the right thing.

If I went into town and was spotted, mine and Bobby's plan would be shot. 'Course, if I didn't go warn Turley, he might end up dead. I felt a shiver as a snowflake landed on my cheek. The shiver wasn't brought on by the snow or even the cold; no, I was thinking about what Lester said.

Now, don't get me wrong, I sure never put any stock in all that stuff about Luther being in any spirit world and sending me a warning from the grave. Naw, all that spooky stuff was for wide-eyed kids. I told myself that over and over, but still I had a few doubts. Locked in this world of flying snow and shadows, it was plumb easy to imagine spooks and goblins of every kind. I can tell you, I was mighty glad when daylight came.

The sun never really came up that morning. It was way too cloudy for that. Instead, the shadows slowly retreated as a pale light spread across the land.

My feet felt like blocks of ice in the stirrups when I finally reached Whiskey City, but even so, I didn't ride straight into town. Instead, I circled wide around the town, aiming to come in behind Turley's old dugout, which was dug into a hillside just outside of town. No smoke came from the chimney, so I didn't reckon Turley was home, but I figured to stop there anyway.

Even if Turley wasn't home, I could stash my horse in his corral and go inside and warm myself a mite. After turning my horse into the corral, I went inside. Despite the fact that the fire was out, the place was warm.

"Leave it to Turley to have the warmest house in town," I said, grumbling and touching the stove. The metal was still warm, like the fire had just gone out. I wondered where Turley might have gone so early in the morning; he wasn't famous for being an early riser.

His coffeepot still sat on the stove and was warm, so I poured myself a cup and walked to the window. Sipping the coffee, I stared out the window and studied the town. There didn't seem to be much going on down there, but I reckon that wasn't all that unusual. With the snow and all, most folks were likely staying inside.

Turley, now he'd likely be in the saloon, and knowing him, he'd be there all day. I thought about just sitting tight and waiting for him to come home, but an impatience was riding me. I figured it wouldn't hurt if I eased into town. If I was careful and with all the folks tucked into their homes, I might be able to do some snooping around without being seen. I might even be able to cut Turley out of the herd, or at the least find out if Lilly had made it into town yet.

My mind made up, I sat my coffee cup down and slipped out of the house. I shot a wistful look at my horse. I sure hated walking.

One thing about it, walking was warmer than riding, but that's the only good thing I can say about it. In fact, I was heating right up when I slipped into Burdett's barn. The place was deserted, which didn't exactly shock me. It didn't take much of an excuse for Burdett to quit working, and a little skiff of snow would do the trick most every time.

On second glance, it came to me that the stable wasn't deserted. Oh, there weren't any people, but the place was crammed to the rafters with horses. The hard-packed yard out front was littered with buggies and rigs of every kind. I recognized most of them and it seemed to me that everybody in the country was in town today. But where were they?

I plopped down on a barrel and scratched my head. If the whole country was gathered in Whiskey City, how come the place looked like a ghost town? Starting to worry, I crossed to the door and looked out through the light snow. I couldn't find any tracks or signs of a struggle, but the snow would have taken care of that. As I gazed down the empty street, a lonely feeling swept over me. It was like everybody just left, or they died.

Feeling like a dog who just lost his master, I stood in the falling snow. Then I saw it, a trickle of smoke rising from the stovepipe in the church.

Now, what the devil was that all about? It wasn't Sunday. The only time anybody ever went in the church during the week was when somebody croaked.

All of a sudden it hit me. They were having a funeral! Somebody had died!

Chapter Twelve

A heavy feeling settling in the pit of my stomach and, my hand resting on the butt of my shooter, I eased down the street. I kept close to the buildings, trying to keep out of sight as much as I could.

At the saloon, I stopped and poked my head inside just to be sure. It would be just like Turley to sneak down here and help himself to a few free snorts while everybody else was at the funeral.

No such luck today—the place was bare. Dragging my feet, I headed on down toward the church. All of a sudden, I didn't want to go there. As long as I didn't know who was dead, I couldn't feel too bad about it.

I reached the church and circled around to the back. Standing by the window, I swabbed at the mist that suddenly fogged up my eyes. Feeling stupid for eavesdropping on a funeral, I walked circles in the snow, my hands jammed down in my pockets.

Finally, I forced myself to wipe the snow from the glass and look inside. Mr. Claude stood at the preaching stand, all gussied up in a stiff black suit. A closed pine box sat in front of him. I could see Mr. Claude's lips moving and hear the low murmur of his voice, but I couldn't make out the words

I wasn't interested in Mr. Claude. I turned my eyes to the crowd, searching for Eddy. I spied her sitting in the front row, and she looked like her whole world had just caved in on her.

Right away, I figured her dad had took a turn for the worse and cashed in his chips. No, there he was a couple of seats down from Eddy. I don't know if his wounds were troubling him or he was just struck with grief, but the man didn't look at all well. As a matter of fact, the whole family didn't look at all well.

I scanned the crowd, looking for the face that was missing. Gid and Iris sat together; low and behold, the old biddy was sniffling a little. Now, she wasn't actually crying. I reckon real tears would dry up and blow away on that wrinkled desert she called a face, but she was red around the eyes.

My eyes went back to the Wiesmulluer family sitting up front, then it dawned on me. Bobby was missing. Betsy sat beside Eddy and both of them had their heads down and were crying. In a flash, I knew it, this was Bobby Stamper's funeral they were having. I knew it, but I didn't want to admit it.

I pulled out my knife and slipped it under the window. If I could pry the window open a little, I might be able to hear the sermon and find out for sure who died. I was so intent on getting that window open that I never even saw the man ghost up behind me. The first clue I had was the gun being shoved into my ribs.

My whole body stiffened as I felt the gun stab me in the back. My eyes looking straight ahead, I gripped my knife ready to use it if the chance arose.

"I'd hate to splatter your guts all over that nice pretty window," a cold, jeering voice said as the barrel of that pistol ground painfully against my spine. I felt him reach around and slide my pistol from the holster. "Toss that frog sticker away, then turn around real slow."

I ground my teeth together, contemplating whirling around and taking a swipe at him. I figured he was gonna kill me anyway and I might as well go down scrapping. Somehow, I just couldn't work up the gumption to do it. With a heavy sigh, I dropped the knife. I figured as long as I was alive, I had a chance. My captor might get careless and give me a chance. As I turned around and looked at him, I knew in an instant this was Nick Oakley and he wouldn't get careless.

He wasn't as tall as me, but he was a blocky, solid-looking man. His thin, pale lips curled into a sneer, looking out of place on his wide, square face. I noticed all of this in passing, but it was his eyes that caught and held my attention. They were cold and gray, and bored into me with an intensity that woulda put a chill in a bonfire.

"You're Nick Oakley!" I blurted out without thinking.

Oakley smiled and nodded. "That's right, and if you've heard of me, you know I wouldn't hesitate to blow your head off."

Now, that there was the gold-plated truth. After all I'd heard about the man, I wondered why he hadn't killed me already. I decided it didn't matter, I'd best just be glad that he hadn't.

Oakley jerked his head down toward the stable. "Take off walking," he ordered.

Having little choice in the matter, I did as he asked, but when I started to turn in the barn, he tapped me none too lightly on the shoulder with the barrel of his pistol. "I never said to go in there. Just keep on walking."

Rubbing my shoulder, which ached from the clout he'd laid on me, I stared back at him in disbelief. What was he going to make me do, walk all the way to Denver? Oakley pointed up at Turley's dugout with his pistol. "Get up to that dugout. There's some old friends waiting to see you. Dying to see you, as a matter of fact."

I had no idea what he was talking about, but I didn't care for the ominous tone in his voice. He didn't give me much time to think about it. He kept shoving me in the back, and by the time we'd reached the dugout, I'd just about had myself a bellyful of that. With a last shove, he pushed me through the door.

As I stumbled inside the dugout, I saw the place was jammed with folks. Seated in the center of the room and looking poised and lovely as a picture was Lilly Simmons. Behind her stood two hard-looking men. I'd never seen either of them before, but from the look of them I knew they was paid fighters. And they looked fit for the job.

Luther lay on one bunk, and despite the fact that he was wounded and obviously in no shape to put up a scrap, his hands were tied. On the other bunk, tied hand and foot and lined up like a bunch of clay pigeons, were Cimarron Bob, Lester, and Elmo.

"Sorry, Teddy. They snuck up on us while we was sleeping," Cimarron Bob said, his old head hanging.

"Shut up, old man!" Lilly snapped, rising from her chair. For a second, I thought she would strike the old man, but instead she just glared contemptuously at him. "Some hired killer you turned out to be. I ought to have Nick kill you right now!" She spat at him.

"Leave him alone. It's me you want," I said. I stared at her, wondering how I'd ever thought she was a desirable woman. Oh, she was still pretty enough and she looked like she'd just stepped out of one of them fancy dress shops back east, but I knew all of that was only skin deep. This was one hard woman, who would trample over any thing or anybody that stood between her and what she wanted. Right now, she wanted that gold mine, and I was the one keeping her from having it. I didn't have to be a genius to figure out what she had in store for me. The laughable thing was, the mine was worthless. Maybe I could make her see that.

"Leave these men out of this," I said, planting my

feet square under me and crossing my arms over my chest. "You're after Turley's gold mine?"

"That's right!" Lilly snapped. She took a step closer to me. "Maybe you're not as dumb as you look. If you sign over the mine, we wouldn't have to kill you."

Now, I wasn't sure I believed that. I opened my mouth to tell her the mine was worthless, then suddenly changed my mind. If she wanted the mine, why not just give it to her? It wasn't worth a plugged nickel and it might give me the time to think my way out of this mess.

"I can't sign over the mine," I said, then hurriedly added, "The deed's over at the bank. I'd have to go get it."

Oakley and Lilly exchanged a glance, and their eyes held for a long time. I held my breath as they thought it over. Finally, Oakley shrugged and leaned against the doorjamb. Lilly took another second to think it over, her face looking like she was chewing on pasture pancakes. "All right," she said through tight lips. "Go get the deed, but just remember we have your friends here. We won't hesitate to kill them."

I nodded grimly and jerked my hat down. I had no idea how I was going to get my hands on that deed, especially since I didn't own the land anymore. I figured in the next couple of minutes, I'd best come up with something mighty slick. I started out the door, but Nick Oakley put out his arm, blocking my path. He pulled out his big silver pocket watch, twirling it as he smiled at me. "Just to make sure you hustle right back and don't get any fancy ideas, you should know that if you ain't back in ten minutes, I'm going to kill big Luther here.'' Oakley smiled at me again, then shoved me out the door. ''Now, hustle along, you sure don't want to be late.''

I stumbled and slipped in the snow. From my knees I glared up at Oakley, and wished all sorts of harm on his head. It didn't seem to bother him any; he just laughed and waved a hand toward town. ''You better scamper, boy, I'm starting to time you now.''

Growling and cussing under my breath, I threw a handful of snow at the ground. With Oakley's laughter ringing in my ears, I trudged down the gentle slope into town. I could see the folks had moved from the church out to the graveyard. I could faintly hear their voices drifting back to me as they sang a hymn.

Nobody took notice of me as I approached the graveyard. They had their heads bowed as Mr. Claude led them in a prayer. Taking off my hat, I walked through the gate, then suddenly stopped short as I saw the name burned into the wooden marker at the head of the open grave. My hat slipped through my numb fingers and my mouth dropped open. My knees went weak and I felt icy fingers claw at my spine. For a moment, I couldn't move, frozen to the spot. The name on that headstone was my own.

''Sweet Jezebel!'' a shrill voice screamed, startling me out of my stupor and nearly shattering my ear-drums. I jerked my head up to see Mrs. Burdett staring white-faced at me, her hand over her mouth. She let out another scream, then staggered backward. For a second, she teetered on the edge, her hands flapping wildly, then she flopped into the open grave.

As one the group turned to face me, looks of disbelief and shock stamped on their faces. They looked like they had just seen a ghost or something.

Eddy pulled away from her mother and took a faltering step toward me. "Teddy!" she whispered, big tears rolling down her face. "Is that really you?"

"Yeah, it's me, all right," I said quietly and took her into my arms. I could feel her body tremble as she sobbed into my chest.

"We heard you were dead," she said. "You'd been missing for days; then, when the stage came to town, Josh Reynolds said two men sent a wire from Central City saying they had killed you and wanted the reward."

I frowned, looking down into her wide black eyes. "Where's Bobby? He was supposed to tell you that I wasn't dead, that this was all just a hoax."

"We don't know where Bobby is. He's been missing almost as long as you," Eddy told me.

Her eyes red, but the rest of her face holding onto a determined, hopeful look, Betsy clutched at my sleeve. "What about Bobby? He is with you, isn't he?" she asked, looking back toward town.

I patted her shoulder and swallowed the lump in my throat. "No, he's not with me. The last time I saw him, he was on his way back to town." I stopped and gazed miserably down at the ground. "Don't you worry, I promise I'll find him." I pulled her close, hugging her and Eddy together.

I looked over the tops of their heads and spotted Mr. Andrews as he and the rest of the men struggled to hoist Mrs. Burdett up out of the grave. "Mr. Andrews, I need to see you over at the bank."

They pulled Mrs. Burdett to safety before Andrews answered, then he shot me a puzzled look. "What's going on?"

"I haven't got time to explain right now," I said, very much aware that the ten minutes Oakley gave me was quickly ticking by. "Let's go over to the bank, I'll explain on the way." I looked down at Betsy and wiped the tears from her face. "Don't you fret, I'm going to find Bobby."

As me and Mr. Andrews headed up to the bank, the rest of the folks just naturally tagged along. "Teddy, what's this all about?" Andrews asked as we passed through the gates of the cemetery.

"Lilly's back and she wants Turley's mine."

"Didn't you tell her that it ain't no good?" Turley demanded.

"Not yet," I answered. "She and Nick Oakley are holding Cimarron Bob, Lester, Elmo, and Luther hostage. She said she was going to kill them if I don't give her the deed to the mine. Since the mine is worthless, I figure to give it to her and see if we can get out of this without any bloodshed."

Andrews was unlocking the door of the bank; now he glanced back at me. "What's the big deal? Those men are all outlaws. Let her kill them, probably be doing the rest of us a big favor."

"That's right, there's no use in the rest of us risking

our lives to protect swine like Elmo and Lester," Iris declared.

"How do you know once she gets her greedy little fingers on that deed that she won't just up and kill the lot of you?" Mr. Claude speculated.

I shrugged; that very thought had been running through my own mind. "I don't, but the way I see it, it's the only chance I have to save those men's lives. I'm hoping once she's got what she wants she'll take it and go."

"You're dreaming, Teddy," Andrews said bluntly as we trudged into the bank. He took a seat behind his desk and placed his elbows on the top. "The minute she gets her hands on that deed, you're as good as dead."

"Dang right," Wiesmulluer bellowed. He straightened up to his full height, holding his left arm around his wounded chest. "We got enough men. Let's storm the place and put an end to this."

"We can't do that!" I cried, trying to reason with them. "If we charge that dugout, she'll kill everybody in there!"

Only hard looks greeted my plea. I guess everyone figured the men Lilly was holding were outlaws, and if she killed them it was only justice. "How about it?" I demanded, whirling back to face Andrews. "Are you going to give me the deed or not?"

Andrews rubbed his chin and squirmed in his chair. "Teddy, I don't . . ."

"I'll give you two hundred dollars for it," I pleaded.

Andrews leaned back in his chair, looking offended, but I knew that was an act. Money never offended Andrews. "Now, see here, Teddy. It isn't the money. I just don't want to see you get yourself killed for a bunch of no-account outlaws."

"I'll give you five hundred!"

Andrews folded his arms and smiled tolerantly. "You don't have that kind of money."

"I'll sign a note," I countered quickly. "You know I'm good for it." .

For a second, I thought he would refuse; then, with a shrug, he pulled a piece of paper from his desk. Writing quickly, he made out the note for five hundred dollars, then shoved it across the desk. While I signed the note, he fished out the deed and signed it over to me.

Pushing the note back, I scooped up the deed and crammed it into my pocket. Eddy grabbed my sleeve. "Teddy, don't do this. I couldn't set through another funeral for you."

I smiled down at her and stroked her cheek, trying to show more confidence than I felt. "Don't worry. Once I give her the deed, I'll explain that if she kills us, she'll have the whole town coming down around her ears. I think if she gets what she wants, she'll leave quietly enough."

Now, even in my wildest dreams, I wasn't sure that was the way it would happen, but that was the only hope I had and I clung onto it with both hands. I bent down and kissed her lightly, then stepped to the door.

"Teddy, you might find a need for this," Andrews said as I reached the door.

As I turned back, he pulled something from his desk and tossed it across the room to me. I snared it out of the air, then opened my hand to look at it. It was a small derringer pistol. "Thanks, Mr. Andrews," I said and slipped the pistol into my coat pocket.

"If we hear a shot, we're gonna come foggin' it up there, so you best grab some floorboards and keep your backside down," Turley promised as he checked the loads in his pistol.

I thanked him again and stepped through the door.

The snow had stopped, but the sky was gray and the day was bleak-looking. I fingered the tiny pistol in my pocket, then started walking slowly. Two shots in that pistol. Not a lot to go up against three tough men and a woman who was meaner than all three of them put together. I'd be lucky if I ever came out of that dugout alive.

Chapter Thirteen

As I rounded the corner of the livery stable, I could see Nick Oakley standing outside the dugout waiting for me. He grinned and pointed to his watch. "You're almost a full minute late," he taunted. "Lucky for your friends that I'm a generous man. If you got that deed, I won't kill them."

"I got it," I growled and pushed past him.

"Give it to me," Oakley said, grabbing my shoulder.

"Not so fast," I said. I threw Oakley's hand from my shoulder and stepped up to the table where Lilly sat. I placed my hands on the table and leaned over, getting nose-to-nose with her. "First, I want to know what happened to Bobby Stamper."

Oakley laughed and pounded his fist against the table. "If you're hoping he will come to your rescue,

148

you can just forget about it. I sent that stuffed hat to his great reward a few days back.'' Oakley laughed again and held his hands as if he were sighting down the barrel of an imaginary rifle. ''It was beautiful. Six hundred yards if it was a step, and bang, one shot,'' he said and clapped his hands together, the sound cracking like a shot. ''He flopped outta the saddle like a rag doll.''

''Enough of this,'' Lilly said, her face as hard as week-old bread. She stepped around the table and held out her hand. ''The deed, give it to me.''

I shrugged and pulled it from my pocket, but I held it out of her reach. ''You went to a lot of trouble for nothing. There's no gold in that mine.''

Lilly smiled and tucked a stray lock of blond hair behind her ear. ''Nice try, but you forget that Turley gave me some gold from that mine.''

''Oh, yeah, sure Turley took some gold from the mine all right, but it was just a small pocket. He cleaned out all the gold before he gave the mine to me. Believe me, that mine isn't worth the price of a drink.''

''Then you won't mind giving it to me,'' Lilly said easily.

''Why not?'' I said with a shrug. I held the deed in my left hand and my right was in my coat pocket, wrapped around that derringer. If they all crowded in close to see the deed, I might have a chance to take them. I flipped the deed down on the table, then took a step back and tensed my muscles, ready to make a play. I was all keyed up to jerk out that tiny pistol and go to blasting if they all crowded in around that deed, but it never happened. Nobody even moved, except for Lilly, who picked up the deed and began to read. "Kill them all!" she said, her voice calm as if she just asked someone to shut the door.

A wolfish grin on his face, Oakley straightened up and slid the gun from his holster. "Hold it!" I screamed and held up my hand. "I can't believe you are going to kill all of us for a mine you know is worthless."

Lilly placed the deed carefully on the table, then looked up at me and smiled sweetly. Now, her face might have looked sweet and beautiful as an angel, but there was an ugliness in her voice. "My dear sheriff, you never did have any brains. That mine is worth a fortune!" She stepped up close and patted my cheek lightly. "You see, when Turley gave me that gold it was straight from the mine, so I had it assayed and they told me all that black rock mixed in with the gold was silver. Very high-grade silver."

I shot a glance at Luther, who lay on the bunk. "That was what you were trying to tell me last night?" I asked, and he nodded weakly.

All of a sudden, Lilly wanted to talk. I reckon she wanted to crow about how clever she had been. "After I found out about the silver, I checked with the man who bought the rest of Turley's gold. He told me every sample of the ore had deposits of high-grade silver mixed with the gold. He said, judging from the samples, there was likely a large vein of silver. He figured there would be more silver than gold."

"Why would he tell you all that? I mean, it wasn't even your mine." I said wonderingly.

Lilly smiled and smoothed her hair. "You'd be surprised what a man will tell to a pretty girl," she said, and slipped gracefully down into her chair. She picked up the deed. "Kill them all," she said, waving the deed in our direction.

"I don't think you want to do that," I said quietly.

"Well, you ain't running this show, so you best say your prayers," Oakley jeered.

"I told the folks in town what's going on up here. If they hear a shot, they're gonna come storming through that door. I don't think you want to take on the whole town."

Oakley laughed. "I ain't feared of that bunch of chicken farmers," he declared, but he slid the gun back into his holster and drew a knife. "But what the hey, I'm flexible."

"I can still holler," I pointed out. "Besides, if you kill us all, them folks aren't going to let you leave."

"I'll take my chances," Oakley said, but Lilly had other ideas.

She glanced up from the deed, a thoughtful expression on her face. "He's right, a few hostages would help us get away. As soon as we get out of this pee-dink town, we can get rid of them."

Now, I didn't much care for the way she said get rid of us. It had a permanent sound that set me to sweating under the collar. "Look, you don't need all of us for hostages. Just take me and let these other fellers go."

"Sure, we could kill them right now," Oakley agreed eagerly.

"You go and kill off half the country and you'll have a devil of a time trying to work your mine. The whole country will be up in arms against you," I informed them.

One of the two men standing behind Lilly licked his lips, then took a step forward. "Look, Nick, maybe he is right. We go to killing this many people and they ain't gonna let us just waltz out of the country."

"Shut up, Grandy!" Oakley snapped. "You and Fred go bring the horses up."

"And don't forget, you're gonna have to come back and work the mine. They'll be just waiting for you," I pressed, sensing that they might be weakening.

Lilly folded the deed and put it in her purse. "We have no intention of working the mine. I already have a buyer lined up," she said, then stood up. "But the sheriff has a point, we won't kill anyone until we have to. Still, we'll take you along just to make sure none of those yokels down there don't get any cute ideas."

"What about Luther?" Oakley asked. "He's half dead anyway."

"Leave him, he'd just slow us down," Lilly commanded as she picked up her cape.

Under iron-gray skies that threatened to dump more snow on us at any time, we rode away from Whiskey City. The townsfolk were lined up in the street, watching us ride off. I hoped someone would go up and check on Luther. The big outlaw was in no shape to make it down to town on his own. At the end of the line, I could see Betsy and Eddy standing together, clinging to each other for support.

I realized that I was going to be the one to have to tell Betsy what happened to Bobby. I wasn't looking forward to that. I could hardly believe he was dead.

As Whiskey City dropped from sight, I shoulda been thinking about saving my hide, but my mind was buzzing with the thought of all that silver. I couldn't forget that I'd just given away the deed to a mine that might be worth a fortune. I found myself staring at the purse looped around Lilly's neck with greed in my eyes. I began to devise all sorts of schemes to spirit it away from her. Most of them were plumb wild and would only get me killed, but I couldn't push them from my mind.

'Course, I found out just how stupid that line of thinking was when Elmo dropped back beside me. "Did you see, she put that deed in her purse. Now, I figure a couple of sharp gents like me and you could snatch that purse and give these galoots the slip."

I groaned, knowing if me and Elmo were thinking along the same lines, I was way off track. "We wouldn't get ten feet," I said irritably.

"Shut up!" Oakley snapped, whacking Elmo over the shoulders with a riding crop. For a second, I thought Elmo would spout off to the gunfighter, but he didn't. Instead, Elmo looked across at me and winked. I rubbed my temples, which were suddenly pounding. That danged fool was liable to get the whole bunch of us kilt.

After that, nobody spoke. The wind began to pick

up, stirring and blowing the snow on the ground. Soon the air was full of snow, as more began to fall from the skies. If anyone from town tried to follow us, they weren't going to have much luck; the snow was wiping our tracks right behind us. Slowly the snow closed in around us, cutting how far we could see to mere yards.

Nick Oakley rode broad-shouldered into the snow, paying no attention whatsoever to the storm. The storm might not have bothered Oakley, but it worried me. I'd growed up in this country and knew that even though it was still very early in the fall, it wasn't a good idea to get caught out in the snow. Many a traveler had lost their way and froze to death in just such a snow.

I noticed Oakley's two henchmen didn't care for the weather either. They kept looking at the sky, then at each other. "Nick, we have to stop and find some shelter," one of them said, his voice pleading.

"Shut up, Grandy," Oakley snapped, without even turning his head.

Now it was plain as a shirt on a sow why they wanted to stop. You never saw a bunch more ill-equipped to deal with cold weather in all your born days. They all wore jackets, but none of them had a warm coat, and if they were carrying supplies, they weren't much. I decided to see if I could worry them a mite more. "You best listen to him, Nick," I said conversationally. "This snow could last for days. We don't find some shelter, we could all freeze to death," I told him and it was true enough.

"Whadda you mean snow for days?" Oakley scoffed. "Why, it's barely October. This little squall will blow over and it will be warm again tomorrow."

"Maybe," I admitted. "And it might set in and snow for a week solid. I seen it happen before."

Grandy tore his eyes from the sky and looked at me. "A week? It couldn't snow that long," he said, but the tone in his voice said that he believed it could and would.

Oakley snorted and spat in the snow. "Don't listen to him. I don't know what he has up his sleeve, but he's trying to spook us. It ain't even cold yet."

Now, I noticed while Oakley was shooting off his mouth about how warm it was, he had his coat cinched up tight under his chin. "It ain't cold yet, but you wait until the sun goes down, it get real cold in a hurry."

On his own, I reckon Oakley woulda kept going no matter what the weather did, just because everybody else wanted to stop if for no other reason. Nick Oakley was a contrary sort of a man. The thing was, Lilly was running the show and she picked that moment to prove it.

"They have a point, I'm very cold. Let's find a place to stop and get warm. If the weather clears, we can go on in the morning."

For a minute, I thought Oakley would set his heels and argue, but finally he shrugged and led off, swinging our course to the west. He took off like he knew right where he was going and that surprised me some. I didn't think he knew this country very well. It took me a minute to figure it out, then I realized he was heading for my place.

We were a couple of miles away from my place when Oakley turned and jerked his head off to the left. "If you want to find your buddy Bobby Stamper he's over there at the bottom of that ravine. 'Course, there ain't no use in looking for him. I reckon he's covered by a foot of snow by now." Laughing harshly, Oakley turned back to the front.

I glanced down in that direction, but the ravine was wide and deep. I couldn't see any sign of Bobby or his body. I didn't doubt what Oakley said, I just had a hard time believing Bobby was dead. He was always so full of life. I marked the spot in my mind, so I could come back for him later.

As the wind kept picking up, everybody rode hunched over, their heads buried down in their collars. Oakley and his men weren't paying any attention to their captives. Oakley kept all of his attention on the trail; the other two were only concerned with keeping warm. Even Lilly had let down her guard. She'd pulled her cape tight around her and draped a blanket over her head.

To my surprise, I noticed she'd taken the purse from off her shoulder and hung it over the saddle horn. As I stared at the purse hanging invitingly close, a crafty feeling crept over me and an idea sprang to mind.

I stuck my hand in my pocket to warm my fingers and to make sure the derringer was still there. Trying not to be obvious, I glanced all about, but nobody was paying me any mind. I looped my reins around my

horse's neck and guided him up closer to Lilly's horse
with my knees.

I pulled the derringer from my pocket, then slapped
the spurs to my horse. As we flashed past Lilly, I
reached out and snagged the purse off her saddle.
Bending low over the saddle horn, I swung my horse
off to the side and urged him to run. Out of the corner
of my eye, I saw Oakley wheel his horse around and
draw his pistol.

For a man whose muscles had to be stiff from the
cold and was bundled up like a shock of feed, he
snatched that pistol awfully fast and shot mighty ac-
curate. He danged near blowed me outta the saddle.
As it was, his bullet passed through my coat where it
bulged up in the back.

Well, he'd showed me he could shoot and hit what
he aimed at, and I didn't have to be hit over the head
to learn my lesson. I sure wasn't of a mind to give
him another whack at me.

I gave my horse another dose of the spurs, then
twisted around and snapped a shot at Oakley. Them
derringers have never been famous for hitting a target
from a distance longer than the width of a poker table
and I was a good twenty yards away, to say nothing
of the fact that my horse was running flat out. Well, I
missed.

I sure did miss, but I made him flinch. By the time
he got ready to shoot again, I was dodging through
the trees and making a hard target of myself. Not that
it bothered Oakley any; he commenced to blazing

away and didn't stop till his shooter stopped banging. Then he settled for cussing at me.

His cuss words did me no harm and neither did his bullets. Not one of them came close to hitting me . . . well, not close enough to worry me much. But when he told his two thugs to go after me, that put a pucker in my drawers. Now, those guys might not have been the swiftest two gents around, but I figured they could kill me just the same.

Don't get me wrong, I wasn't just running blind. No, sir, I'd devised myself a plan. To this day, I still swear that plan shoulda worked, but it didn't.

It started well enough, I got away clean. Oh, Oakley's two goons were chasing me. I could hear them bumbling and crashing in the bush behind me, but I had every intention of giving them the slip. After that, I figured to backtrack and find Bobby's body.

Now, Bobby Stamper had always been a man who believed in packing plenty of shootin' irons. Most times he had two or three on him. I figured after I found his body and got my hands on them guns, then I was going hunting a man. To be downright truthful, I was going to kill Mr. Nick Oakley, and I didn't figure to shed any tears over his body. He'd killed the best friend I ever did have, and he was gonna pay.

Me and that horse were crashing down the side of that ravine, going down like water over a fall when it happened. About halfway down, my horse stumbled, then fell. We tumbled down that slope and for a while it was horse hooves and boot heels flying every which way.

Despite all the bumping and jarring, I didn't seem to be slowing down until I crashed headfirst into a snowbank. By the time I pulled my head out and got to my feet, my fool horse was on his feet as well. Not only that, he was running away like he had firecrackers in his diapers. Swearing and kicking snow, I watched him run away.

Before I had a chance to think about what I was gonna do next, I heard Oakley's hired thugs coming down the slope. I still had that derringer in my hand, but I only had one shot left. One shot, and I'd have to be mighty close to be sure I hit one of them—a bunch closer than I wanted to be.

Plumb desperate, I looked all about me for a place to hide, but there wasn't any. I had to face up to it, they had me. I just hoped they would stop and ask questions before they commenced to blazing away.

Chapter Fourteen

Through the swirling snow, I could barely make them out; they were just vague shapes careening down that snowy slope. I dropped flat into the snow, clutching that derringer as I hoped—no, make that prayed—that they wouldn't spot me.

Not that I had much hope of that. Even in this poor visibility, there wasn't much way they could miss me. Not unless the good Lord struck them blind, and if he took the notion, I was hoping he walloped them a good one.

Well, somebody up there musta been looking out for me, 'cause them two fellers spotted my horse going over the next hump and they chased after it. I reckon they couldn't tell that the horse didn't have a rider, 'cause they never even wasted a glance in my direction.

After they thundered past me, I climbed slowly to my feet. For a second, I was right relieved and plumb happy to be alive, then I took notice of the raw wind whistling up my backside. My spirits sunk like a rock in a swimming hole. Here I was afoot in what was turning out to be a humdinger of a blizzard.

If I didn't cabbage onto some shelter soon, I was a goner. Not only that, I needed some food. My belly was already growling like a sick bear, and I knew that a man walking in cold weather needed a lot of groceries to keep going.

Well, wishing and worrying wasn't going to get me what I needed, and I knew Oakley's men would nab my horse pretty quick. Once they did, they would start backtracking looking for me, and I best be gone.

I knew where there was a cave that would offer shelter, but I didn't head there. Instead, I followed the ravine, back to the spot where Oakley said Bobby Stamper's body lay.

I was betting that after he shot Bobby, Oakley never bothered to go down and take Bobby's guns. 'Course, I was betting my life on the fact that I could find Bobby and that he still had his guns.

Once I had them guns I figured to be on more even terms.

First thing I had to do was get them guns. I was in a powerful hurry, but hurrying in the snow, which was starting to pile up, was out of the question. I had to settle for slogging along, and believe me, it was hard work. When I finally reached the spot where Oakley said Bobby lay, I started walking in circles, making a wider swing each time. I looked high and low, here and yon, but I never found Bobby.

A glimmer of hope began to build in me—maybe Bobby wasn't dead after all. It wasn't much of a hope, because deep down, I knew the reason I hadn't found him was because he was buried somewhere under the snow. Besides, if he was alive, he shoulda turned up somewhere by now. If he was wounded and out in this weather, he was as good as dead.

Not that my own situation was much better. I was on foot and just about at the end of my rope stamina-wise. I had no supplies and my words about the weather were coming back to haunt me. Right now, it looked like it might snow forever.

My clothes were soaked plumb through and my teeth were chattering like a bunch of biddies at a tea party. I needed to find some shelter and get a fire going.

I knew I should give up the hunt and hustle to some shelter, but I couldn't do it. All of a sudden, I was obsessed with finding Bobby. It wasn't just finding the guns, although I had a powerful hankering to have them in my paws, but that wasn't what drove me to keep hunting. I felt like I would be betraying Bobby's memory if I just left him lying in the snow.

Finally, I had to give up. It was growing dark and the visibility was down to yards. I was afraid, if I kept walking around in circles, I would wind up losing my bearings and that wouldn't be good.

Well, like every other good idea I ever had, I got this one just a mite late. Now, I ain't admitting for a second that I was lost, but I had to stop and ponder a bit. Now, I knew the wind had been blowing straight out of the north, but that didn't feel right. I would have sworn it was now blowing from the west.

Hemming and hawing, I turned three complete circles, but I couldn't find any landmarks that I recognized. Fact is, I couldn't see much at all. The shapes I could make out in the vague swirling light looked strange and out of place. It was cold standing there, so I finally decided that the wind must be out of the northwest. Using that for a guide, I started out.

Well, either the wind was wrong or my brain was gummed up from the cold, cause that cave wasn't where I reckoned it should be. A feeling of panic rushed over me as I stared at the bare wall of the ravine. I tried to force down the panic; the thing I had to do was stop a moment and consider.

I knew that cave was bored into the wall of this ravine. The question was, was it down to the right or up to the left? If the wind was straight out of the north, the cave would be to the right. If the wind had switched more than I thought and was coming out of the west, the cave would be to the left.

I've known folks that coulda set down and figured their way outta this, but not me. Thinking and worrying just makes me nervous. Right then I decided to trust my instincts. A man riding wild country develops a feel for such things, and right now that feel was screaming for me to go left.

Well, I up and turned left, and I found slogging through the deep snow along the wall of the ravine a tough task. After an hour of bucking the knee-deep snow, I knew my instincts had been dead wrong and I'd picked the wrong direction. I dropped to the ground, the breath whistling in and out of my mouth.

Right then I was froze plumb to the bone and dog-tired. To tell the truth, I was ready to give up and cash in my chips right then and there. Lying flat on my back, I gazed up at the falling snow. Half buried in the snow and shielded from the wind, it was much warmer. My body began to relax and I was content just to lie there.

As I lay there, I began to see a light above me, winking and twinkling. For a long time, I stared at that light trying to figure out what it was. Then it hit me. That light was coming from the very cave I'd been looking for. Somebody was up there and they had themselves a fire.

Feeling the power surge back to my muscles I sat up. Now, I didn't know if the people in that cave were friend or foe and right then I didn't care. If they had a fire, they might be cooking and that cave would be warm.

For a little food and warmth, I was ready to take on the whole Seventh Cavalry. And in the mood I was in, I felt like I could whip them too. Hitching up my wet britches, I started climbing up to that cave.

Well, by the time I'd climbed up to that cave, some of the starch had seeped out of my shorts, but even so, I was going inside. If there was food and warmth in there, I meant to have my share.

With that derringer gripped in my big fist, I leaped

into that cave. I came in with a rush, skidding to a halt in the middle. I swept that cave with my eyes, the barrel of that pistol following my eyes. When I saw the man lying in the back of the cave, I was so shocked I dropped that pistol.

"You," I whispered as the derringer clattered to the stone floor. My jaw sagged down to my belt buckle and it took me a minute to get it in working order. "I thought you was dead," I finally managed to blurt out.

Bobby Stamper grinned weakly up at me. "I wondered about that a few times myself," he answered. Grimacing, he hitched himself into a sitting position, then leaned back against the wall. "I sure am glad to see you," he added wryly.

"What happened? Oakley allowed as how he'd killed you," I said, practically climbing into the fire.

"He sure did try, but he missed," Bobby said and shook his head as he laughed. "I was riding along, not paying any attention, when wham, a bullet hit the saddle horn. Well, I jumped backward and that fool horse jumped forward, and you might say we up and parted company. Next thing I knew, I was rolling down the side of that ravine. When I stopped rolling my leg was up by my ear and I knew it had to busted."

"You set it yourself?" I asked, looking at the rough splints around his left leg. Bobby grinned and nodded, while I whistled softly. "That couldn't have been easy."

Bobby shrugged and tossed a few more sticks on the fire. "I ground a couple of inches off my teeth before I got the job done. 'Course, that was plumb easy compared to dragging my carcass up to this cave." Now, I bet that was true. To tell the truth, I don't know how he got either job done, but one thing I've found out about Bobby Stamper is that when he takes a notion, he can be a downright resourceful man. "You don't have any grub on you, do you?" he asked, a note of eagerness in his voice.

"No," I said and shook my head sadly. I knew Bobby had to be almost starving and I was feeling a mite peaked myself.

Bobby gave me a look like a kid who just found out there ain't no Santy Claus and lay back down. "I reckon I can hold out until we get out of here tomorrow."

Now, I didn't have the heart to tell him I was afoot and had no way to pack him outta here. Bobby closed his eyes and went to sleep as I tried to dry out my duds. As I worked my brain thawed out and began to hum again. In good weather, maybe, I coulda packed him outta here, but in this snow, it was impossible. No two ways about it, we had to have some horses.

The only place within walking distance where there were horses was my place. Well, at least I figured there were horses there. I felt real sure that's where Oakley and Lilly were holed up.

If I could sneak over there and swipe their horses, they'd be tied to my cabin—at least till the weather cleared. By that time, I might be able to haul Bobby into town and round up some reinforcements. We might be able to settle this thing for good.

I surely did like the notion, but there was one drawback. If I slipped up and went and got myself killed or captured, Bobby was as good as dead. On his own, he'd never be able to climb out of this ravine. And the chances of somebody finding him before he starved or froze was about the same as me flapping my arms and taking off flying.

Still, if I minded my p's and q's, I reckoned I could pull the job off. One thing I had going for me was Bobby himself. I swear, that boy was luckier than an outhouse rat. Nick Oakley shot at him and missed, and I heard Oakley never missed. If Bobby's survival depended on me pulling this off, I figured Lady Luck would be riding on my shoulder. I guess I came to the decision in a roundabout way, but I up and made up my mind to have a go at it.

While my clothes finished drying, I hunted around that cave for Bobby's guns. I found them tucked into a dry corner. I gave them the once-over to make sure they hadn't gotten wet, but they were fine. Bobby Stamper was a man who took right good care of his guns.

I went to buckle the gunbelt around my waist; then saw I had a problem. That danged Bobby was skinnier than a fence post and his belt was a mite small. I shook my head, then sucked in a deep breath and cinched the thing around my waist. I got 'er buckled, but it didn't ride around my hips like it was supposed to. The dang thing was up around my belly, nearly cutting me in half.

I eased out the breath, more than a little afraid the belt would bust. The belt held, but it felt like it was gonna pop the hat off my head and blow the boots off my feet. The spare pistol I rammed down in my jeans, then I reached for my coat. I glanced back at Bobby, who was sleeping like a bear in the wintertime. Casting off the pangs of guilt I felt over leaving him alone, I slipped on my coat and buttoned it tight.

I stepped around the fire to the mouth of the cave. Now, let me tell you, it took all the get up and go I had to leave the relative warmth of this here cave and step back out into the wind and snow. But I knew I had to do this, so I rounded up all the gumption I had and stepped outside.

Right away, the wind slapped me in the face, and I realized it had gotten colder. Maybe it was my imagination, but it didn't seem to be snowing as hard, and I could almost imagine that I could see farther.

Even so, I moved slow and careful, having found out how easy it was to get all turned around on a night like this. I calculated it was between two and three miles to my cabin. Most times, a body could lope that far in an hour easy. Tonight, I figured it would take at least two, and likely nearer three. 'Course, if I got turned around and lost, it might just take a lifetime— mine.

As I stumbled through the night, a fear haunted me—the fear that I would lose my way and end up wandering in circles. Many a pilgrim had perished in this country that very way. To battle the fear, I put all my concentration on the trail.

As time wore on, and the steps fell behind me with agonizing slowness, the fear pushed harder at my mind and was harder to shove away. Perhaps I'd already come too far. If I'd gotten off track, I could wander right past the cabin and never see it.

The fear kept rising up inside me and threatened to overwhelm me. My head was about to fly off my neck, the way I kept looking from side to side, hoping for something I recognized. It took almost all my will-power to keep my feet from breaking into a run.

My poor nerves had been through a bunch today and were just about frazzled out. It shames me to own up to it, but I was ready to give in to the panic, when I came suddenly into the clearing where my cabin sat.

Right away, I dropped to the ground and ran my eyeballs over the place. Nothing was moving, but that didn't surprise me. It was late and cold, I imagined they were all inside sleeping.

I knew I should circle the place and sniff things out, but I was froze plumb to death. The only thing I wanted was to get them horses and scoot back to the cave and get warm. Upshot of it was, I got up and scatted over to the lean-to, which served as a barn.

With all the horses crammed inside, the lean-to was a sight warmer than outside, although still plenty nippy. A horse raised his head and nuzzled my side. Even through the gloom, I recognized my own horse. "Glad to see me, boy?" I whispered and rubbed be-tween his eyes.

"I don't know about him, but I'm sure glad to see you!" Nick Oakley said, his voice ominous.

Chapter Fifteen

I glanced back over my shoulder and saw Oakley and his man, the one called Grandy, standing in the door of the lean-to. Oakley had his pistol out and headed my way. "Why don't you shed that little popgun?" Oakley asked.

Seething inside, I pulled Andrews's little pistol from my coat pocket and tossed it on the ground. I was furious at myself. I'd gotten careless and now it was time to pay the piper. The worst of it was that I wasn't the only one who would have to pay.

The second that little pistol thumped to the ground, Oakley's whole manner changed. He let his pistol fall to his side and leaned casually against the wall of the lean-to. "You're a pretty smart boy. That was mighty slick the way you got away from us," he said.

I didn't answer, I only stared at him and tried to

figure out what he was up to. Oakley didn't strike me as the type to go in for a lot of loose-mouthed talk. I reckoned he was up to something. I just couldn't figure out what.

"Yes, sir, you dang near made it, till you lost your horse. When the boys came back with your horse, I got to thinking. A smart young feller like you, with more brass than brains, he'd come here and try to steal a horse." Oakley laughed and I could tell he was enjoying himself. "You're a canny one all right, but then I'm pretty sharp myself. I figured out what you'd do next."

"Yeah, you're real smart," I said with a growl. I was miserable as a drownded rat. All of this work and fussin' and we were right back where we started.

Oakley didn't even let on like he heard me. He laughed and shook his head. "You're a born trouble-maker, that's for sure." He snapped his pistol back up. "Maybe I best just kill you right now, and save a heap of trouble later."

Well, that jerked me up short. I went from feeling sorry for myself to using my noggin for something other than keeping my ears from growing together. Right then, I was glad Bobby's gunbelt was so small. The way it rode up around my belly kept it from showing out the bottom of my heavy coat. Oakley didn't know I had the guns, and I had to stall him until I got a chance to use them.

"Go ahead. Kill me!" I taunted and laughed at him. "You kill me and you won't get that deed."

"You ain't got it with you?"

"Nope. Believe me, you could look till you're old as Noah and you wouldn't find it," I said, feeling more than a little bit smug. I took a chance and lowered my hands and turned around.

Oakley was thinking and not really paying any mind to me. He used the muzzle of his shooter to push back his hat and scratched his jaw with his other hand. "You don't miss a trick, do you?" he mumbled. He shuttled his eyes over toward Grandy, who was looking back at the cabin with longing in his eyes. I reckon Grandy was more concerned with getting back inside where it was warm than confabbing with me and Oakley. Oakley looked at Grandy for a long time, then shifted his attention back to me. "Maybe me and you should be partners."

"I got the deed. I don't need you," I replied.

"Oh, but you do," Oakley countered. He smiled confidently and something about that grin made the hair on the back of my neck stand up. Still smiling, he turned and shot Grandy through the head!

The horses, startled by the sudden noise, began to pitch and mill around as I took an involuntary step at Oakley. He whipped the gun over to cover me. "Easy, big man," he warned as the horses slowly settled back down. He glanced at Grandy's lifeless body, then nudged it with the toe of his boot.

"What did you do that for?" I asked, my mind racing as it tried to figure out what he had up his sleeve.

Oakley shrugged. "It came to me that I got way too

many partners. I figure for this deal, two is about right. What do you say, me and you?''

''No, thanks,'' I replied curtly and glanced pointedly at Grandy. ''I don't care for the way you treat your partners.''

Oakley laughed and reloaded his weapon. ''Men like Fred and Grandy are born to be used and discarded when you've done with them. They're only good for something when you're leading them by the nose and telling them what to do. They got no gumption. Me and you, though, we're different. If we was to tie up together, there's no telling what we could do.'' Oakley grinned at me, expecting some kind of an answer. ''If your worried about Fred, don't. I'll take care of him.''

''What about Lilly?'' I asked, stalling for time. I didn't believe him for a second. We'd be partners and friends right up till the time I told him where the deed was. Then he'd kill me as quick as he did Grandy.

''Lilly—now there's a woman,'' he said, and I could smell a trace of fondness in his voice. ''Now, Lilly is a right entertaining lady to have around, if you know what I mean. But she has her heart set on that mine. I reckon I'll have to deal with her too.''

''You mean you'd kill her?''

''Sure, why not? There's plenty of women in the world. A couple of rich fellers like me and you wouldn't have any trouble finding them.'' He grinned, his big, square teeth flashing as he fished a fat cigar out of his vest pocket. ''Well, what do you say? We'd split everything right down the middle, of course.''

"I've already got a partner. Bobby Stamper," I said stiffly.

Oakley lit the cigar, then waved the match out in front of his face. "I took care of your partner the same way I'm gonna do mine. Stamper's dead, I told you that. I shot him myself."

"No, you missed. He's alive and well. Right now, he's in that stand of trees in front of the house with a rifle. I reckon he heard that shot and is wondering what happened. If you was to step out of this barn, he'd think you killed me and fill you full of holes."

With his left hand, Oakley took the cigar out of his mouth as the smug look drained off his face. He shifted his feet and took a couple of nervous glances back over his shoulder. I held my breath, and for a heartbeat, I thought he was gonna fall for it. Then, all of a sudden, his whole manner changed and the smile sprang back to his face. "You're bluffing!" he declared and stabbed at me with his cigar.

"Am I?" I asked, trying to keep the disappointment from showing on my face or sounding in my voice. "Why don't you poke your head outside and see," I dared, hoping he wouldn't want to take the chance.

"Sure," he replied. "Why, I'll even do you one better." He backed completely out of the stable, raised his hands over his head and turned a circle. Laughing, he strolled casually back inside. "I reckon he must have snow in his eyes."

"Maybe, or maybe he's waiting to see what happened to your pal there," I said, pointing to Grandy's body.

Nick Oakley laughed and slapped me on the back. "You don't give up easy. I admire that. But you see, if ol' Bobby Stamper was bellied down out there with a rifle, he'd killed me and Grandy when we followed you in here. He coulda done that real easy. Besides, if he were still alive that would mean I missed, and I never miss." Oakley grinned and held out his hand. "What you say? Partners?"

"I got the deed and you got nothing I want," I stated flatly as I stared coldly at his extended hand.

Oakley didn't get mad. On the contrary, he smiled even harder. "Oh, but you're wrong. Don't be forgetting about that houseful of your friends I got inside."

I shrugged and snorted. "They're not my friends. They already caused me a world of grief."

Oakley took the cigar out of his mouth and let out a booming laugh. "Boy, if we are going to be partners, you're gonna have to learn not to get all weepy over a bunch of goonie-eyed saps. And we're gonna have to learn you how to lie." He stuck the cigar back in his mouth and poked his gun down in the holster, then slipped an arm around my shoulders. "What you say we go inside where it's warm and get this partnership off on the right foot. I tell you what, just to show you that you can trust me, I'll let your friends go."

"If you do that, how can you be sure I'll tell you where the deed is?"

"Them, they's suckers, they ain't important. I'll bet your own hide is a sight more valuable—to you anyway."

"You kill me and you'll never get your hands on that mine."

He grinned around his cigar and squeezed my shoulder. "Teddy, Teddy. We're gonna be partners. I wouldn't kill you and I know you wouldn't hold out on your pard. 'Course, if you were to have a change of heart and decide to get greedy . . ." Nick took the cigar out of his mouth and blew smoke in my face. "Well, let's just say that there's lots of places to shoot a man that won't kill him. I reckon, you'll come around before I run out of bullets." Having spoke his piece, Nick started dragging me out of the barn.

I went along willingly. Not because I believed him, because I surely didn't. I just wanted to get inside and get warm. Besides, Oakley might just up and keep his word and let my friends go. He would if it suited his purposes. Either way, I could get warm.

Lilly looked up sharply as we came through the door. "Where's Grandy?" she demanded.

Oakley crossed to the fireplace and picked up the coffeepot. "Teddy here is a quick lad. He killed Grandy 'fore I could get him cornered."

"Why didn't you just kill him?" Lilly asked as Nick calmly poured two cups of coffee.

Nick handed me a cup and took a sip from the other. "He don't got the deed. He stashed it somewhere." Taking another sip of coffee, Oakley shot a glance at Lester, Elmo, and old Cimarron Bob. "You three, go out and saddle all the horses and bring them up to the house."

They didn't move right away. First, they looked at

each other, then at me. "Don't look at him, go!" Oakley roared.

I gave them a nod and they hustled out the door. I really doubted if they would be back. I figured once they got their horses, they'd skedaddle. Or at least I hoped they would.

To my surprise, they brought the horses up to the house and came back inside. "How come you guys came back? You had a chance to hightail it." I asked, confused.

For a second, they looked shocked that I would even suggest such a thing. It was Cimarron Bob who spoke up. "Shoot, boy, we wasn't about to turn tail and run away, leaving you in a lurch."

"Very touching," Oakley said with a sneer. He pulled out his gun and pointed at the three.

"You promised to let them go!" I flared as I started to unbutton my coat.

"So I did." Oakley waved his gun in the direction of the door. "Get. I don't care where you go, but if I see you hanging around here, I'll kill you on sight."

"No!" Lilly's voice rang out sharply. She had a small .32 pistol in her hand to back up what she said. That pistol, looking big in her dainty hand, was aimed right at Oakley's head. "Put your gun away and sit down, Nick. I'm in charge here."

For a second, I thought Oakley would argue with her. But then he smiled and holstered his weapon. Taking up his cup again, he dropped into a chair.

Her gun still trained on Nick, Lilly flicked a glance

at me out of the corner of her eyes. "Now, Sheriff, tell me where the deed is."

"You let them go and I'll tell you," I said, hoping to reason with her.

"I don't think so," Lilly said, her face hard as nails. "Fred, shoot the old man." Fred drew his gun and aimed it at Cimarron Bob.

"Wait!" I screamed. "I have the deed!" I said and reached inside my coat. Instead of that deed, I hauled out the pistol I had tucked behind my belt. It wasn't what you would call a smooth draw. The bottom two buttons on my coat were still fastened and that gun hung up on the way out. With brute force, I jerked the weapon into the clear. A piece of my coat hung off the front sight as I headed that hogleg at Fred.

His eyes nearly bulging out of his head, Fred tried to swing his gun around at me, but he was a mite late. I squeezed the trigger and my bullet smashed him back against the wall.

All around me, the room seemed to burst apart with motion. As I fired a second shot at Fred, I saw Oakley power smoothly out of his chair, his hand sweeping for his pistol.

Out of the corner of my eye, I saw Lester and Elmo make a clumsy dive at Lilly. I heard them fall and cuss, but I couldn't afford to look and see what was happening. I had to trust them to take care of her, and believe me, that wasn't a very comforting thought. I had no choice as Oakley already had his gun out and aimed at me. I was whipping my pistol around, but I could tell it wasn't gonna be swift enough.

Old Cimarron Bob saved my bacon. He slammed into Oakley and tried to rassle the gunfighter to the ground. As they fought, I heard Oakley's gun go off, but the bullet didn't come near me. I trained my pistol on Oakley, but I couldn't fire for fear of hitting old Bob.

Growling and snapping like a wolf in a trap, Oakley flung Bob away. He was fixin' to take a shot at the old man when I reacted. Taking careful aim, I fired. My bullet humped Oakley solid, but it didn't put him down. Lips pulled back in a snarl, he started to bring his gun to bear on me. Wanting no more to do with him, I fired my last two shots.

Them bullets knocked all the fight and sass outta Mr. Oakley. He raised up on his toes, the gun spilling from his fingers. He clutched his belly and looked at me. I swear, if he woulda had the strength, he would have smiled. "We shoulda been partners. There's no end to the things we coulda done together," he said, then did a nosedive into the floor.

Taking a deep breath, I glanced around and took stock. Lester and Elmo lay side by side on the floor and they weren't moving. The door stood wide open and Lilly was gone. Outside, I heard the sound of a horse running away and I lunged to foller her. I stopped dead in my tracks as I saw Cimarron Bob.

The old gunfighter sat propped up against the wall, staring in wonderment at the blood on his hands. "I've been shot!" he said slowly. "In my whole life, I never been shot before."

"Does it hurt much?" I asked as I lay my gun on the floor and knelt beside him.

He gave me a disgusted look "Dang, boy, I've been shot! 'Course it hurts. It's supposed to hurt."

"I wonder what happened to them two?" I asked, jerking my head at Lester and Elmo.

Bob chuckled. "They was rassling with Lilly—well, mostly they was fighting each other—and she broke away from them. When she headed for the door, they jumped after her and sorta ran their heads together."

I smiled. If they hurt their heads, they were in no danger. "I reckon they'll be fine. I best get you fixed up then go after Lilly."

"I wouldn't bother on either account," Cimarron Bob said gruffly. "I seen enough folks shot in my time to know all the fixing and frettin' in the world ain't gonna do me no good. As for Lilly, she ain't gonna make it far, not in this weather. The best thing you can do is let her be."

I looked out the door, thinking maybe he was right. What if I did happen to catch Lilly and she put up a fight? Well, I knew I'd never feel right if I had to kill her. Besides, I needed to take care of Bob. All of a sudden, I wanted him to live. I wanted it real bad.

Trying to imitate what I'd seen Turley do for Mr. Wiesmulluer, I went to work. As Cimarron Bob grumbled that I was wasting my time, I heard Lester and Elmo stirring behind me. They stumbled over to us and stood over me with a lump apiece on their foreheads.

"C.B., you cain't die," Lester wailed, sniffling like an elephant with a runny nose. "You promised to teach us how to rob a train."

Old Bob looked up at them, a kindly smile on his weathered face. "Boys, if I were you, I'd forget about outlawin' and go straight. I don't reckon the West is ready for a couple of desperadoes like you."

"Yes, sir," they both mumbled, holding their hats in their hands while I wound a bandage around Bob's chest.

Cimarron Bob grabbed my hands in his. "Boy, I want you to take good care of that gal of yours. She's a mighty fine young lady. Yes, sir, mighty fine."

"I'll do my best," I promised, my eyes burning like chili powder.

He smiled wistfully. "I sure wish I coulda found a lady like her. Things might have turned out different." He started coughing, and for a while, I didn't think he would ever stop. Finally he did, but when he spoke again, his voice was very weak. "Tell that girl, if she thinks about it from time to time, to put a flower on my grave. I surely would admire that," he said, and that was the last thing he ever did say. He let out a sigh and just seemed to melt away on us.

As I stared down at his body, I thought about what folks always said about him. They said that he was a mighty mean man and that he done some terrible things in his life. Now, I reckon there's some truth in them words, for I know Cimarron Bob Williams weren't no angel. Not by any stretch of the imagination.

But the way I see it, he gave his life to save another and that sorta evens things out. I figure a man should be judged for the way he ends his life, not for the things he done in the middle. Cimarron Bob ended his life helping others. And that's the way I'd like him to be remembered.